NIGHT'S LIES

GESUALDO BUFALINO was born at Comiso, Sicily, in 1920. He studied literature at Catania and Palermo, and was a teacher by profession, turning author only after his retirement in 1976. He started his first novel, *The Plague-Sower*, in 1950, but it was only in 1981, after taking the discarded manuscript out of the drawer and reworking it, that it was published; it won the Premio Campiello. This has been followed by a succession of remarkable novels and other works, including *Blind Argus* ("a construct of time and memory, artful, and full of delight" *Scotsman*) on which the translator, Patrick Creagh, has won the John Florio Prize. With this novel, *Night's Lies*, the author won Italy's top literary award, the Premio Strega. A volume of his short stories and his novel *The Plague-Sower* are also to be published by Harvill.

D0658452

By the same author

BLIND ARGUS

Gesualdo Bufalino

NIGHT'S LIES

Translated from the Italian by
Patrick Creagh

HARVILL
An Imprint of HarperCollins*Publishers*

First published in Italy with the title *Le menzogne della notte*
by Bompiani editore, Milan, in 1988
First published in Great Britain
by Collins Harvill in 1990
This edition first published in 1991
by Harvill
an imprint of HarperCollins Publishers,
77/85 Fulham Palace Road,
Hammersmith, London W6 8JB

9 8 7 6 5 4 3 2 1

BRITISH LIBRARY CATALOGUING IN PUBLICATION DATA

Bufalino, Gesualdo
Night's lies.
I. Title
823′.914 [F]

ISBN 0-00-271122-2

Photoset in Linotron Galliard by
Rowland Phototypesetting Ltd, Bury St Edmunds, Suffolk
Printed and bound in Great Britain by
HarperCollins Book Manufacturing, Glasgow

Contents

TO

The Two of Us

ONE

The Place

They ate little or nothing. The food, though more palatable than usual, since a well-meaning warder had done his best to spice it up, had a hostile taste to it, and not a morsel but turned to ashes in their mouths. Loss of appetite is, of course, the rule on evenings of farewell. The execution being fixed for first light on the morrow, the baron became increasingly heated over the hypocrisy of serving condemned men unwanted delicacies while not scrupling to poison them with the reminder of their imminent decease.

"We shall not make a good death on an empty stomach however," he sighed. "At such an early hour in the morning, too, when the light is at its most exhilarating . . ."

Saglimbeni, in one of his frequent flights of poesy, backed him up.

"Sunset, indeed, would be a more felicitous hour. With that half-mourning, those drooping clouds, those crimson and violet shadows that benignly shepherd one on towards quietus. Done in this fashion we shall consider ourselves the victims of an intolerable eviction . . ."

The soldier said not a word, and appeared to be inspecting his boots. He had turned up the collar of his jacket, as if to ward off the cold. It was Narcissus who spoke: "Morning or evening, what's the difference?" he blurted out and, with small consideration for the others, burst into tears.

*

The fortress is the sole inhabited site in the island. It is known as an island but ought to be called a rock. For it is nothing more than a stack of volcanic tufas heaped up into the form of an enormous snout, wearisomely steep in places, but for the most part bare, sheer crag. The strip of sea between it and the mainland is no wider than a keen eye can traverse. None the less to cross it, be it through the malice of the winds or of the currents, is a hazardous business for vessels, and totally beyond the power of any swimmer. No one is ever known to have escaped but their remains have been recovered, glaired with seaweed and mauled by fish on the rocks of the Black Foreland.

The perimeter of the place is but half a league, or thereabouts. Where a fistful of soil permits, savory and capers flourish, born of sparse seeds carried on the wind. No grazing there, except for the almost milkless goats and a herd of ownerless donkeys roaming the seashore at the foot of the Needles; and the icy month of January nightlong hears their doleful braying . . .

As by a tortuous path you clamber up, your eye embraces on the one hand the immensity of the open sea, an infinite reach of blue to the western horizon; on the other, beyond the neck of water, there is the mainland, where you glimpse a harbour, a crescent of dwarf houses; but neither man nor motion. Also deserted is the sky, but for a lone bird winging its way from the island to the Kingdom, bearer of occult messages.

When finally, after zigzagging back and forth, you have gained the summit, that snout we spoke of is abruptly lopped off to form a platform, wherefrom arise the mighty bastions of the fortress, a squatness of solid granite, nicked only by the entrance-gate. Past which – though not before men-at-arms have ordered you to halt and demanded the password – if you drag your now weary feet on across the cobbles the grating of the hinges has not ceased at your back but an inscription above an archivolt, with its unyielding couplet, brings you both terror and comfort:

Donec sancta Themis scelerum tot monstra catenis
vincta tenet, stat res, stat tuta tibi domus.

You are still brooding upon the meaning of this as you traverse the courtyard, at one moment taking care to step round the holes in the paving which drain off the rainwater, at another observing the little chapel set in its midst, and reserved for the sacred functions so necessary in a situation where one is alive by sheer accident and the chances of death are legion: be it the chronic dysentery which ravages the inmates, or the savagery of one's companions, so quick to fly to the knife, or else the sentence of death, imposed at the discretion of the Governor even for trifling offences.

At the four corners of the quadrangle are as many sentry-boxes to shelter the guards in foul weather; at night it is illuminated by eight gas lamp-posts. Even so, the head warder has more than once complained of a remaining scrap of shadow, propitious to dirty doings.

"Let them break out, if they've got the guts," says the Quartermaster. "So many mouths the less for us to feed. And so much offal for the sharks."

Speaking more generally and fancifully, the lay-out of the edifice somewhat resembles the pincers of a scorpion, their tips almost touching, barely leaving space for a gateway. Cast up your eyes from here towards the keep, and see the walls rise sheer, with a hundred loopholes containing a hundred secrets, and a hundred spectral faces peering forth, all curious about the new intake.

"A Pompeian residence," was Saglimbeni's quip as he passed beneath the portcullis. "Backs to the world, we enjoy

11

the fine view of the comforts within. A Sans-Souci, in short: a holiday home for Persons of Rank . . ."

The registrar, relieving his bladder a step or two away, took offence without having followed his meaning, and came to tighten the shackles around their index fingers and thumbs. Besides, it only took five minutes for the prisoner, sampling the force of the sun on the lead-covered slopes of the roof, to realize that he was, give or take a level or two in Dante's Inferno, in the pit of it.

The rooms on the ground floor are reached by way of a pillared loggia, and serve for various purposes both civil and military. Should we wish to become acquainted with them, to pass them under review, the first we happen upon is the guardroom, with its rowdy voices and stools and racks and tackle; then the armoury, pompously known as "the arsenal"; beyond this the carpenter's shop, the forge, and the discipline room (which in all truth is the torture chamber), and the sick-bay, which includes the doctor's surgery; then the laundry room, heavy with the tang of hessian, the bakery or grub-shop, the kitchen (or "griddle"), the so-called company office, the latrines, and the garrison quarters. Finally, the head of a flight of seven sunken steps leading to a low, underground door confining an incurable halfwit who at the dawn of every day, in imitation of a rooster, emits a strident "cock-a-doodle-doo!"

The Governor's quarters form the first floor of an entire wing; but he, a long-time widower and valetudinarian, has willingly restricted himself to three rooms, leaving the others adjoining to his officers. A kindness dictated by expediency, the aim being to disguise the most indiscreet inspections as courtesy visits. Be that as it may, his apartments are distinguished by the two banners fluttering from the balconies: the white standard bearing the royal lilies, and the regimental banner depicting a black griffon on a shield surrounded by the names of famous victories.

Epic recollections, but in no wise impressive to the sparrows who have chosen the flagpoles as perches to rest on before flitting up to chirrup at the gratings. Here, on the sills, a handful of crumbs awaits them at each dawn of day, scattered there by the inmates to assuage their loneliness. Thence, rendered bold and tame, they slip through the bars of the most friendly of the cells and even peck from someone's palm, or hop about on a shaven pate, or inquisitively investigate the miserable furnishings . . . Until the blue sky calls them, and they take to the wing again, they who may, into the open spaces.

The cells, a word about the cells.

Murky oblongs with a single aperture high up, reached by using another's hands as a stirrup but affording only a scanty view below, the embrasure being sloped up at such an angle as almost to preclude it.

The floor measures thirteen spans by seventeen and contains (counted one by one to pass the time) fifty-one slabs of pitch, which excesses of either heat or cold cause to sweat strangely. Four plank beds, propped against the wall during daylight hours and lowered at dusk, two on each side. Between them, a viable gangway, an evening battlefield where in the winking of an eye the most immoderate emotions clash and run wild: black rages and reckless false hopes.

A perpetual oil-lamp, just sufficient to illumine the roll of the dice, hangs from a peg rammed into the wall. Above it a figure of the Virgin of Succour, glued together with spittle and bread-dough, listens alternately to prayers and vituperations. Blackened by smoke, what's more, and a lodging house for tiny spiders spared rather from laziness than compassion.

Damp walls and peeling plaster, handy for breaking off a

13

flake to play at drawing figures on the floor. Unless you might prefer, without assurance of ever finishing it, to weave a straw hat from the stuffing of the palliasses . . .

As for fittings, they are sparse: four blocks of stone to sit on, set into the floor lest they be used as weapons; in one corner a terracotta urn covered with graffiti of hearts and daggers; an oaken door with iron bolts and a peephole for constant spying and check-ups, along with a hatch, opening from the outside, for the passing to and fro both of the mess-tin of mush and the chamber-pot of excrement. The emptying of which into tubs slung from a pair of wooden shafts is not, we might add, carried out by warders or other military personnel, but by a handful of civilians guilty of the bloodless and less atrocious crimes, and happy, despite the repulsiveness of the job, to be able to stretch their legs along the interminable corridors and to exchange a few words with their less fortunate companions. Now and again they undertake to act as couriers between the latter, which in the eyes of the law is an unforgivable crime; and not infrequently they pay the price face to face with a volley of musketry. This has earned the Governor the nickname of "Sparafucile" – Old Trigger-happy – after that operatic bass-part that is all the rage just now.

No news, up here, of the king or of the Kingdom. All they know from taps on the walls, as from distant drums, is that the queen has delivered a stillborn heir, and that therefore were the king to die . . .

They are also kept informed of the sea, from the clamour of it, in rough weather, against the rock base of the island. They know, too, of the sky; what they see of it chequer-boarded through the bars of the air vent, as it shifts from shade to shade, flesh-hued, or grey, or pearly, according to the passing of the hours or the seasons. They know of the stars and the paths they take; of a cloud that came every midday for months, like a resolute hope, only to dissolve of a sudden as a ribbon comes adrift in the hair of a little girl running; a cloud that vanished, eventually, never to appear again. They know that across the sea someone is still thinking of them, because they are allowed (hypocritical generosity!) to receive gifts once a month: pipe tobacco, a change of underwear, the wherewithal for coffee, a polyglot Bible. Even a brass inkpot, on one occasion. Incongruous for two reasons: because it was devoid of ink, and writing was forbidden anyway . . . They know, above all, that the powers that be have not forgotten them, but are slowly grinding away, behind distant desks, to achieve a result in terms of signatures and sealing wax (a buzzing in the ear denotes its approach) which is the very estuary of their life on earth.

In the meanwhile they dream of the Kingdom, of the highways, the woods, the fertile plains where now and again, as they passed on horseback, they saw a solitary ox at the plough, and behind it a slender, girlish figure, bare-legged, a kerchief knotted about her blond head, and she waved a greeting, and they waved back, and it was like kissing . . . And the odeums, the theatres with a thousand lights bestrewn upon the streets, the women's faces in the lobby, aglow with health and youth, the waltzes, the fluttering fans, the carriages, the farewells that sought each other out in the crowd before the crack of a whip sundered destinies in darkness . . . and the raging joy of being alive, of feeling the whole of one's body aflow with pulsing blood, warm with unfailing warmth, bursting with words and tales to tell; harmonious, and perhaps immortal!

In the depth of night they wake, first one and then another, alerted by a signal in their heads, an alarm which has not been deceived by any friendly moon, but persists in reminding each of them, with the precision of a pendulum clock, of the

15

number of days, hours and minutes of life remaining to them. It awakens them, and the first damp glimmer of sunlight always catches them thus, staring at the ceiling, their eyes half sealed with dreams and half with fear, intent on tracing lines of force and dispersion among the beams, a network of escape routes, hatchways, loopholes, through which they achieve a joyous weightlessness, an aerial insanity, a sensation of flight which in their unwritten, unspoken idiom corresponds, so virginal and pure, to the idea of freedom.

TWO

Who, Why, and Wherefore

As to who the four men are, and how they have been reduced to their present predicament, the Governor, Consalvo De Ritis, is refreshing his memory by the light of a candle, between one bout and the next of his wasting disease. He does not, to this end, consult the immense library of records and depositions in which the conspiracy is dealt with at length, but rather, with his sole remaining eye, scans an imposing volume and reads the dossier of each of them, compiled by the efficacious pen of an assistant and now lacking nothing for its perfection but the Amen of a final date.

If we read them over his shoulder, these dossiers run as follows.

CORRADO INGAFÙ, Baron of Letojanni, known to his intimates as Didymus, is a person of a certain age, of medium height, sluggish in body. His face is long, bearded, and emaciated; his hair brown, though flecked with white. To all appearances of a gentle character, beneath the surface he is prone to the most monstrous and iniquitous designs. Of noble family, for many a year he resided in idleness at court, until the day when, gripped by a frenzy of hatred towards his equals, he went astray.

Thereupon, following in the footsteps of other hotheads, he took to travelling beyond the Alps, where he is said to have contracted the plague of sectarianism, and whence he returned with a strange and joysome air, and highly loquacious, whereas previously he had preferred to hold his tongue. Not long passed before he found himself outlawed and, enrolled in the band that had set the country aflame, growing therein so inveterate as to become lieutenant to that secret chief whom they call *God the Father*.

Many years he spent thus in the forests and on the highways, hardened malefactor and assassin, and forever stirring up the lower orders with promises of transitory relief. Hard of discovery, so shrewd was he at moving with his band from region to region, aided by his rapport with the disaffected of the place, and not disdaining a number of dens in the capital city itself, creeping thence with vulpine stealth to the detriment of the Crown.

One clue betrays him, although to gain direct evidence of it would require lengthy association with him: that he is most singularly disturbed by storms. To the point of moaning and hiding in cupboards, after the manner of a little boy. The which should be made known to all innkeepers, that they may hold it suspicious in the case of a guest unknown to them.

In another hand and in more recent ink

Apprehended in the crowd on the 7th day of February, immediately after the massacre, he himself seared by a splinter from the infernal machine and with garments still reeking of gunpowder. Guilty by confession of *lèse-majesté*, he was condemned by the Court of the Vicaria to the fourth degree of public example, in date the 12th day of October.

The sentence to be carried out in the fortress, by means of decapitation, on . . .

SAGLIMBENI, self-styled poet, is among the most mysterious of the insurgents, even his real name being unknown. He seems a man of forty or so. As for his origins, some say he is a Corsican from Ajaccio, others a Neapolitan from Casamicciola. By profession, some say printer, others teacher. He is universally dubbed poet for being the author of verse lampoons against the Throne and the Altar, which pass for gospel-truth on the tongues of the common people.

He has a suave and copious way with words, persuasive to wrongdoing. In physique he is well set and good looking, though touching on the corpulent; his mien is benevolent, with a full and ruddy complexion and an ever-laughing eye. Round of face, he is no hairier than a woman; womanish also is the minute care of his person on which he insists even in an extreme emergency. Tales are told of this which smack of the incredible. Of how, on finding himself surrounded by the militia, with warning ample enough to have given them the slip, he told his barber in no wise to stop dressing his hair, and escaped for all that over the rooftops with audacious leaps.

An imposing adventurer if ever there was one. We cite an example: one day he feigned readiness to make reparation, and delivered himself up to Justice Sbezzi, promising a full confession in the judge's private apartments. Whence, having blinded the Justice with pepper in the act of offering him his snuffbox, he escaped scot-free disguised as a woman.

A lover of music, he is accustomed to frequent auditoriums and theatre-lobbies, disseminating cockades and subversive leaflets. It is in places such as these that the criminal police are adviced to seek him out.

In another hand and in more recent ink

Apprehended three days after the massacre, on the steps of the Opera House, the evening of the performance of *Gli Orazi e Curiazi*.

Guilty by confession of *lèse-majesté*, he was condemned by

the Court of the Vicaria to the fourth degree of public example, in date the 12th day of October.

The sentence to be carried out in the fortress, by means of decapitation, on . . .

AGESILAOS DEGLI INCERTI, soldier, thirty years of age. Of bastard birth, deposited by a mother unknown on the revolving hatch of a convent, he was brought up in an orphanage and appeared to be destined for the Church but, at about sixteen years, for no apparent reason he ran away and, spuriously claiming to be older than he was enlisted in the army under an assumed name. Thus he took part in the late war in Macedonia, with the rank of grenadier; though it happened that, out of contempt for obedience, having conceived a loathing for an officer, he flew into such a passion against him as to deprive him of life, and, having done so, to mutilate him foully of his genitals; thereafter making good his escape from his fetters during the turmoil of an enemy assault. Nor was he further heard of except here, in the Kingdom, for having disarmed the Municipal Police in three towns and thrown open the gaols, always in the rout of Baron Ingafù, whose humble adherent he is said to be.

Volatile of mood, veering from the most boyish optimism to the direst dejection; of a circuitous cast of mind, delighting in every kind of cavilling argument, whether on God, the State, the nature of Man . . . but always in the form of painful sophism, from which he extracts a variety of stimuli, now to bestial ferocities, now to arcane pieties. On account of his long-standing skill with fuses, mines, and similar artefacts of sulphur and saltpetre, he is presumed to be the principal artificer of the device which exploded, with so much bloodshed, beneath the Royal Stand on the day of the Jubilee, February the Seventh. Broad faced, doe-eyed, his stature is above average. He may be recognized by the tattoo of an insect which, after the manner of sailors, he bears on his arm.

In another hand and in more recent ink

Apprehended on the 9th day of February in the hostelry to which he had fled after the massacre.

Guilty by confession of *lèse-majesté*, he was condemned by the Court of the Vicaria to the fourth degree of public example, in date the 12th day of October.

The sentence to be carried out in the fortress, by means of decapitation, on . . .

NARCISSUS LUCIFORA, student. Of indeterminate age though youthful in appearance, albeit possibly less so than he seems. From his earliest years he seethed with mutinous feelings towards any authority whatever, either in heaven or on earth, ridiculing them in public, not only in the streets and cafés, but frequently during religious processions and rites.

A devout worshipper of Venus, aided and abetted by being a fine figure of a man, of outstanding strength and attractiveness. At once delicate and strong-limbed, like a Hercules Apollo, he is square shouldered and slender-legged, with curly dark-brown hair, though he wears it shaven short at the nape. Accomplice and sedulous ape of Saglimbeni, he is at his side in any hazardous assay, and has succeeded thus, though still of tender years, in being accepted into the Cabal, and becoming a member of the Republican Directory, which they by way of jest call the Holy Office, and which acts as intermediary between the hidden Chief and the disciples.

The last time he was set eyes on at close quarters he was in the act of leaving Palazzo Linares, to which he had gained entry through a ground-floor window, whether to steal the valuables or to pay court to a woman is not known. When pursued, he made his escape with a flash of speed. Beneath his dustcoat of flowered indienne he was, at the time, wearing

21

a dark blue shirt and woollen breeches, and was shod in light, city shoes.

In another hand and in more recent ink

Apprehended in the crowd on the 7th day of February, in the company of the baron. He carried on his person large sheets of paper strewn with Arabic numerals, resembling a secret code. Interrogated upon which, he said in his defence that they were jottings to aid his memory, he being utterly addicted to the game of Lotto. Later on, while in various ways mocking the Clerk of the Court, he declared that they were love letters of immodest import, which he would never think of deciphering, in deference to the politeness of our ears . . .

Guilty by confession of *lèse-majesté*, he was condemned by the Court of the Vicaria to the fourth degree of public example, in date the 12th day of October.

The sentence to be carried out in the fortress, by means of decapitation, on . . .

The Governor has grown weary of reading. He is lying athwart the ottoman fully dressed and with his boots on; the toe-caps of which seem to him miles away, those of another, of some dead soul . . . He peers at them with his single eye, and round the edges he thinks he discerns two or three caked splashes of mud. ("How early winter has come," he thinks. "Balestra will hear about this . . . He's been slacking for quite a while, that rogue . . . O God, the agony in my head! I'm not long for this world . . .") With the other eye, the one beneath the bandage, he stares at immutable blackness, where for thirty years has dwelt the second, the truer, half of existence. He would like to summon Balestra, but his voice is too weak to call. He therefore grabs the bell on the table next to him and agitates it till his orderly appears, his face all false solicitude; a snub-nosed, nondescript face that will live

22

heavens knows how much longer than his own. What's the point of hauling him over the coals? He gives up the idea, and simply asks for his monocle and the portfolio on the desk, bidding him place it on the stool beside his couch. ("God, what agony!" he thinks. "There's a rat in the marrow of my bones. I'm not long for this world"); and he raises the monocle to his good eye.

From the portfolio he draws a folded paper resembling the others, though bound about with a distinctive ligature. Before he has time to undo this he is struck by a fresh paroxysm wrenching his mouth askew, while the room becomes misty, the walls recede . . .

He is walking through an old garden, between banks of oleander. The air around him is languid and aromatic. The pathway is so narrow that only one may pass, and this stirs in him a sense of security and happiness, as long ago in games of hide-and-seek. He moves towards a face that is waiting for him, the face of his wife as it was at their first meeting, at the Lancers' Ball; a radiant face, small, eager, betwixt two wafts of a fan. "Kiss me," he hears on the instant, and runs towards the kiss; but beneath his lips he feels those others tumefy into scabs and ulcers. He breaks away in horror; shadow swallows up her hunchbacked form. But not before she has cried out, "Some day I'll pay you back for this!" And, from afar, she makes a strangling gesture, as if to throttle him.

Now the ground gives way beneath his feet. Now he is falling in a fury of black flashes, headlong into a deep trap, a well swollen with rains, reddened with wine or blood, he knows not which, where finally among wild splashings he goes under . . . A kick with the heel just brings him to the surface. He swims with strong strokes, but the broader they are the further down he sinks . . . Then, drenched in sweat, but nothing worse, he wakes.

"Sacred Heart! Sacred Heart of Jesus!" His prayer is soundless as his nails rip desperately at the buttons of his tunic. The braided frogs resist a little; he wrenches them off.

The fang of agony does not cease to gnaw him. No, this cannot be some fortuitous disorder of recalcitrant tissues. More likely the fruit of some malignant purpose. He bites on a hand, softly, without sinking his teeth in; with the other he undoes his breeches, exposes his groin to the air, as if that might bring him some relief. Yes, someone, be it God, be it rat, is laying plots against him and deliberately alternating agony with armistice. The best strategy will be to go along with it, accustom himself to living with the pain, making it part and parcel of his daily timetable.

Unless it would be better to fall to his prayers . . .

He reaccustoms his lips to the muttering of a prayer, from time out of mind draws up the first few words.

"Our Father," he murmurs, "which art in heaven . . ." But he gets no further, for his thoughts fly off at a tangent towards the shadow of another "Father", the unknown *God the Father* shielded by the four about to die.

He smiles a bloodless smile. "Each of you has perfect health," he thinks, "but you will die before I do."

He unties the document, fixes in his monocle, and in the tones of a bureaucrat starts to read again.

NOTATION OF OUTLAWRY
Against a Person Unknown
commonly known as
GOD THE FATHER

The prime mover and master of the conspiracy, presiding over its conclaves and manipulating its strings from obscurity, he it is, according to both secret information and common opinion who, disguised, approves the novices and, with a bodkin, administers the blood-sworn oath. He it is who gives the passwords and the orders, issues instructions for missions and designates the victims.

He is known in person only to the four members of the Holy Office, or Committee, called the Four Evangelists, and so shackled are they to him by bonds of superstition as to venerate him as *God the Father*, whence has arisen his popular nickname. Nor have they consented to say more, though urged to it by the most pressing forms of torture. Nevertheless, on the word of an informer who claimed to have eavesdropped on him in the dark, we may know of his voice that it is calorous with flatteries and spurious encouragements, but that at times, whether it be from a genuine defect or an affectation, it breaks into a stammer.

A rumour, purposely spread in order to defame persons of rank, has it that he is of excellent family, among the first in the Kingdom; but an inveterate gambler and laden with debts. Nor would we wish to suppress another calumny still more distressing and absurd, come surreptitiously to the ear of this office by anonymous letters: that, in order to learn his identity, it would be enough to . . .

There follows upon this an illegible smudge, and the Governor grimaces.

"Clerk of the Court," he says out loud, "you are the soul of prudence. First to write something in accordance with your duty, and then to blot it out as if it burnt your fingers. Unless you too have a touch of damn liberalism in you, as one might suspect from the whiskers on your chin . . ."

In the meantime the pain has abated. All that is left of it now is a bruised, tender feeling like a small boy's hurt, in need of kissing and fussing over. He can get to his feet, and does so. He swiftly readjusts the bandage over his sightless eye and crosses to the desk, where he adds a number of lines of his own to the document, which he then folds and returns to its place. Finally he makes a brief, close scrutiny of himself in the mirror on the dressing-table, as if hoping to discover some secret in that face of his, and with an old man's gait he leaves the room.

THREE

Negotiations

The warder Licciardello had arrived with genial step, his bunch of keys jangling on his belly. He had not expected, having given the lock its three turns, to find the prisoners seated as before, each with his bowl of food on his lap, still intact. Intact, but never to be served up again, he noted with mild regret, since they had sprinkled the contents with ash and doused the stubs of their last cigars in them.

He left the door ajar behind him, and advanced with a certain circumspection. Too often he had heard of "patients" who, having nothing more to lose, had revenged themselves on their gaolers with their bare hands. Therefore at his belt he carried a rawhide whip, and had arranged for an armed sentry to be stationed in the passage, alerted to enter at the double at the slightest cry.

"All gone to waste! Such a gift of God, too!" he declared, without addressing anyone in particular, as he removed the dishes from the hands of the four men and emptied them nonchalantly into a tub on wheels which he pushed in front of him like a wheelbarrow.

The four men were seated on their stone stools, already arrayed for tomorrow's gala in coarse canvas uniforms as prickly as a monk's habit from head to foot. They had, as was their wont, stuffed rags under the bolts of their fetters, to prevent them from biting into the flesh of their ankles, and sat there motionless and silent, answering not a word to the man's comments.

But as he persisted in nagging them cheekily with "You'll be hungry during the night. Time passes slowly on your last night's vigil," the baron waved him away with an imperious gesture.

The man moved off towards the door, but turned.

"The barber'll be round later on to crop your heads," he said. "No need for you to go out, or him to come in. Put your heads out one by one through the hatch."

In melancholy tones Saglimbeni addressed Narcissus. "These locks will soon be shorn away, O Phaedo," he quoted, stroking the lad's head with a fatherly hand.

But a babble of voices and clatter of boots was heard in the corridor.

The Governor thrust open the door and entered. His height was such that he had to stoop a little. A wrinkling of the nose immediately made it plain that the stench of heterogeneous sweat long absorbed by the walls was distasteful to him. In the same instant, through the door they caught a glimpse behind him of the glittering weapons of his escort picket, while the original sentry pressed himself to attention against the wall.

Licciardello was taken aback by this unheralded visit, and havered between his obligation to salute and the propriety of hiding from sight the tub of muck which he was wheeling.

But the Governor snapped, "Get out of here, you! Everyone out!" And he emphasized his words with a gesture. "I wish to be alone with the prisoners." Then he kicked the door shut on the dim light from the corridor.

The four had remained immobile, but in their hearts they were far from uncaring. Of their visitor they were familiar, of course, with the figure, the nickname, and the reputation;

not so the voice, having set eyes on him, ashen faced and silent, only while they were on the rack. But that in these desperate straits, in which any novelty could only be a change for the better, as the worst cannot be worsened . . . That he had now gone to the lengths of paying them a visit, and dared to be with them in the absence of any kind of escort, well, it gave them a tingling in the veins and a feeling of turmoil which, if one were to give it a name, could only be called "hope".

Nevertheless – although the unexpected offering which this man had in his grasp might even have been a royal pardon – as if by mutual consent they all assumed an air of indifference, and waited in silence for some word or gesture. There ticked away a minute, or maybe two. Time to take stock of this Governor face to face. Almost a giant of a man, with reddish beard and moustaches, though the crown of his head, where not already moth-eaten with patches of alopecia, was strangely whitened. A foreigner, from the look of him, and had it not been for his indigenous name one might have taken him for a Swiss or German, descended hither from the Alps to seek his fortune. A man at arms, reduced by his infirmities to an exile on this islet, there maintaining the illusions and ramrod pride of *la vie militaire*, indulging in frequent war-games and wearying the garrison with defence strategies and anti-invasion manoeuvres. Unfailingly, he chose the hour of the midday meal to summon his general staff to his couch of pain.

So much for the outward show. But many another tale was told of him, of exploits far more cunning and more cruel, dating back to the time of the siege of Scútari. Rumour had it that his present hypochondria broke out in him after the death of his well-beloved wife, worsening with the encroachment of that decay which for years now had been eating away his bones. No denying, though, that when he was not in pain and had slept well, it was still possible to hear from his lips statements of an astuteness and profundity more suited to a philosopher than to a man of arms.

The four men knew this, and therefore, not without some lightening of the spirit, they waited for him to speak.

They remained seated, with his standing figure looming above them. And he began:

"As that ancient Roman did to Carthage, in a fold of my toga I bring you war or peace, life or death. I know your stoutness of heart and I admire it. Not everyone can keep his lips stubbornly sealed under physical torture. But where rack and thumbscrew have been of no avail, the pact which I put before you may possibly succeed. For this time it is not a question of choosing between death and dishonour, but between two different kinds of dishonour, one of which will lead you to live, the other to perish."

He pulled himself up abruptly, biting his lip.

"Forgive me. I have read too much among the ancient historians. Less abstrusely then, and more bluntly, I say to you 'Tell me the name of your leader.' I am not asking you, you understand, to betray an idea, but only a man. And this in such a manner that whoever does betray will remain incognito, not only to his fellows but also to me, and will have no cause for shame except towards himself, in the secrecy of his heart. A shame easily forgotten, if I know the hearts of men. In exchange, and in the name of His Majesty the King, whose extramural lieutenant I am, I promise immediate pardon for every man of you, exile to the Argentine colonies, and in your own time, when calm has been restored, repatriation."

He received no reply, but continued:

"The night is before you. Eight long hours in which to consider which suits you the more: saving your skins or an illusion of glory. Assuming that you accept this pact, you will proceed in this wise. It is the custom that the last vigil of condemned men be spent without fetters, and not in the prisoners' cells, but in the confessional chapel where the padre is even now awaiting you. Shortly, when you arrive there, you will find a fifth guest bidden to tomorrow's festivities, comfortable beds for all, and four blank sheets of paper on a table. Whenever you wish, though I advise the last possible moment, each of you, in secret from the others, will either inscribe a cross, which denotes refusal, or else the name I ask you for. These you will slip into a slotted box. Tomorrow morning, on my return, should I find four crosses you will die. If, alternatively, on even one of the sheets, penned by an anonymous hand, the name is revealed, all four of you will go free and no one will know who was the traitor."

At this point the baron spat on the ground before him. The others instantly followed his example.

"I would have hoped," said Sparafucile impassively, "for some sublime response, such as might have become proverbial. For example, *Pete, non dolet*, or *Summum crede nefas animam praeferre pudori* . . . Or, lacking that, a somewhat drier retort," he added, smearing the spittle into the floor with the sole of his boot.

"Be that as it may," he continued, "this trial is so contrived that there is no escaping from it. For by shirking it you would admit to doubt in your own steadfastness, and if not in the letter, at least in the spirit, play traitor. True courage is not a public display of communal heroism, yelling your own lukewarm convictions in competition with all around. That way I have seen men die in battle by the thousand, like sheep, shoulder to shoulder in squares around the flag. It will be true courage to withstand the temptation when no one is watching, and you are alone in the silences of your own conscience; to reject pardon and, instead of the name I ask for, to write, if you dare, an arrogant, unanimous NO.

Otherwise you will mount the scaffold with a viper of doubt in your bosoms, accusing yourselves of cowardice and maddened at dying to no purpose."

A lengthy pause ensued, and then the baron all of a sudden burst out "He's right!"

"He's right," he said. "I have heard tell of a saint who must needs sleep between two naked nuns before he could be sure of having vanquished the temptations of the flesh. Just so our end will only be crowned with glory if we dispel all misgiving."

Hampered by his irons, he rose to his feet with some difficulty, and craned his neck to look up at the Governor.

"Sir," he said, "merchant in bloodshed, is it permitted, in lieu of a mere cross, to inscribe some more trenchant curse?"

The Governor remained unruffled.

"I venture to think, on the contrary, that at least one of you will be wise enough to decide to live. Place these two things in the balance and you will find no comparison. On the one hand is the light, the wellspring of light; the chance to say 'I was, I am, I will be'; the chance to be, still, a unique drop in the ocean of existence; to take a woman's body in your arms, to sniff at a flower, to laugh, to cry, and at every moment to say 'Me, Me, Me . . .'

"That is one side of the scales, and it is mountainously weighty. On the other side, however, there is only a whiff of impalpable nothingness, the shadow-land of all and sundry, where your words Equality, Liberty, Fraternity, which seem to you so inevitable today, will have no minds to think them, hands to write them, tongues to utter them . . ."

He broke off suddenly, and his azure eye for a moment clouded over. The rat had stirred in his head, taken a gnaw or two, then dozed off, or pretended to.

"But you," asked Saglimbeni, "you who torture and kill, do you therefore think your cause more just than ours?"

"Yes," replied the Governor wearily. "Not so much because it defends a monarch and his worldly claims, but because above all thrones whatever it sees shining the blazon of God."

"Even if the monarch is a tyrant?" exploded the student.

"Even a contumacious pope," was the reply, "remains for all that the Vicar of Christ. Just as the best of your sort will always be a sycophant of Satan."

The soldier was on him at a bound, encircling him with arms like hoops of steel, though without doing him injury.

"Shall I make mincemeat of him?" he quietly enquired of the baron.

A mere glance of reproof sufficed for him to release his hold and return to his seat. The Governor had paled beneath the touch of rouge tinting his cheekbones. Recovering himself, he hissed, "I am seventy years old, but only last year I could have struck you dead in a flash."

He then turned to the others, speaking in tones intended to sound oracular.

"Yes, there are only two vicars of God upon earth, pope and king; whereas you are thousands upon thousands of clowns and flunkies of the devil; and you call yourselves the people; and you steal forward in hiding; and you have laid a mine in the earth that with a single blast will demolish the paragons of the ancient world, the precedents of experience, the laws and the enactments of every assembly and senate . . . A mine that goes by the name of *The Rights of Man*."

Saglimbeni gaped. "And you, you old fossil, would like to deprive us of them? In the name of what?"

"I see all of you," replied the old man, "as an error of calculation on the abacus of Creation. To punish you is my ecstasy and my damnation. To punish you, to cure you, to purge away the excess and error which you are. For if you yearn for martyrdom, as at Holy Communion the believer yearns for the Host, my joy it is to be its executor. I am

Justice and Punishment, a naked sword, the executioner and surgeon of Providence. Upon this blood-bathed globe, where all that lives must be ceaselessly immolated even until the end of time, until the death of death . . ."

"These words," grumbled the baron audibly, "are someone else's, and I know whose . . . You do too much reading, Sparafucile . . ."

The latter gave no sign of having heard him, but continued: "I am not expecting to win you over, if well-soaked lashing rods were not sufficient to damp your ardour. I come merely to propose a pact, and in exchange for one man to render you your lives. This name – not that of a *God the Father* but of a genuine Antichrist – one of you will tell me, if he finds it in his heart to do so. In which case, at this time tomorrow you will all be aboard a vessel bound for the Atlantic. If not, you will be merest nothing: four corpses and four heads in a sack on the seabed . . ."

"You're counting your chickens before they're hatched," jibed the poet, while the Governor, clicking his heels in some attempt at a military leave-taking, moved with bowed head in the direction of the doorway.

"I shall visit you again in your new cell tomorrow at dawn," he said on his way out. "When I come to unseal the box."

"Have no fear, we will be at home," was the baron's little joke.

But by this time the barber was calling through the hatch, "Poke your heads out boys, one at a time! Through here, that's it. I won't take long, I'm swift of hand. Most of the cutting is up to my senior colleague, tomorrow morning . . ."

Agesilaos was the first to go forward, with a docility strange in him. The others watched his giant body bend, and a forest of tough bristles succumb, beyond the door, to a pair of invisible sheers.

FOUR

Decisions on
How to Spend the Night

At the consolatory chapel "of no return" they arrive in single file, with an armed escort under the command of a sergeant. Not, however, before being released from their irons and admitted to the little shower-room, where they are permitted to undress and wash, with the aid of coarse black soap and buckets of water poured by unseen hands through a hole in the ceiling. Well-towelled and fresh, but freezing, since they have been flayed of the protective dirt which for months has served them for a skin, the four men find themselves in their new lodgings, patrons for a single night and ill-disposed to sleep it out. And more averse still to undergoing a further cleansing from Father Turlà, the confessor, whose assistance they reject so energetically as to put him to flight for ever.

Left on their own, they look around to familiarize themselves with the room. It is a space between two and three times as large as their former den, reasonably clean, and aired by two windows out of which it is possible to see. There is a touch of perfidy here, however, since what comes into view is that portion of the yard where the scaffold is being erected.

Lining the two longer walls, three and three, are beds, each one surmounted by a crucifix and all unoccupied save one, on which huddles a bundle apparently asleep, resembling the dummies escaping prisoners hide between the sheets to bamboozle the warders. Only that this is quite clearly living flesh, its head swathed in a panoply of bandages stained with dried blood.

"Brother Cirillo," the sergeant informs them on his way out, jerking a thumb at the inert bundle. "He'll be keeping you company twice over, here for tonight and tomorrow in hell." And the door closes behind him.

The four of them eye the other with some awe, not daring to disturb him. All their lives they have heard talk of that fearsome old man, having even at one point discussed among themselves whether they ought not to draw him into their ranks to aid the common struggle. A God-fearing, sanguinary brigand, known jestingly as "Brother" in imitation of Michele Pezza, half a century or more ago, whom they nicknamed Fra Diavolo. He had lived on the run for forty years, looting and pillaging the countryside. Of vast intelligence, he was said to be, and by no means ignoble birth; one who, when assailing a monastery of some great country house, even before searching for victuals or valuables would ransack the library for books to read in the leisured days of winter, there in the gorges of Lagopesole where he and his band made their lair.

That he had at last been taken, and, what is more, alive, word had recently passed around the fortress, transmitted from wall to wall by tapping knuckles, rising storey by storey until it reached the cells of the political prisoners; but that he was immured in their midst, and his head destined for the very same basket, was a fresh discovery, though of small import to men by now devoid of curiosity.

The condemned men throw themselves down on their bunks and close their eyes. No, not to sleep, (it goes without saying that they will steal a little extra life by staying awake all night), but because of certain pangs in the pit of the stomach which have come upon them only now, after their ablutions, and which, when all is said and done, they recognize as fear. It is a sort of encumbrance they confusedly feel knotting in their gut, becoming a body within the body. In the same way, perhaps, a woman first becomes aware, in the silence of the night, of the faint stirrings of the child she is carrying. Except the prisoners find this burden of growing flesh painful; a subterranean tumour which, like the rat in the Governor's head, every so often awakes and sets its teeth into them.

They are afraid, all four. They would be less so, perhaps, had they been left in their former cell. But all these recent and unaccustomed happenings – the shaving of their heads, the ablutions, the change of quarters – have broken that lukewarm timelessness in which until now they have all but lost awareness, and tolled the conclusive knell of the event hanging over them. Until today death has seemed no more than a bit of stage business to be acted ere long, on the tacit understanding that as soon as the applause and bowing was over they would all retire into the wings, get dressed, and be themselves again. Whereas now, point-blank, they find that they will no longer be themselves, they will no longer be anything at all, and in their minds they plumb the depth of the impending darkness . . . But what am I saying, darkness? The dark is a kind of blindness, in which nevertheless one fumbling hand can grasp another, and you can walk together, united in remembering and lamenting the light . . . But death is neither light nor darkness, only abolished memory, total annulment and non-being, an incineration with no residue, where everything that was is not only no longer, nor will ever be again, but is as if it had never been . . . They are afraid. Yes, afraid every one of them, and they stretch out, the three older men on the one side, the student on the other, leaving the unoccupied bed between his and the friar's. Hearing them enter the latter does no more than open a wide eye from amid the bandages, and then fall back into his stony stupor.

The room is too dazzling, with the glow of the evening

striking through the windows added to the glare of four torches affixed in iron rings, and then the little flamelet beneath a holy image. To the point that Agesilaos, after the manner of mowers sheltering under a hedge from the midday sun, knots the corners of his kerchief and drapes it over his face. Then he tires of the game, throws the thing off and looks about him again.

Thus by common accord they endure an hour stretched on their bunks, their gaze fixed on the objects on the table in the middle of the ample room: the writing materials, the slips of paper, the ballot-box or Mouth of Truth, with a slit on one side like an alms-box in a church, and locked as a guarantee of secrecy. All, in fact, as promised by Sparafucile.

Until the baron rises to his feet and with a questioning "Well, shall we get this off our minds?" approaches the table. Here, before dipping his pen in the ink, he pauses and addresses the others: "Or would it not be better to wait until tomorrow morning, as agreed?"

And he moves back to his place.

As do his three companions, who have risen in his wake, avoiding each other's eyes and hoping, we may well imagine, that one of them at least will be a coward on the morrow, but all despairing that any one, alone, will dare to be so.

At this point Cirillo, emerging painfully from his rags: "What's going on? Who are you? What is all this?"

He appeared too lethargic to grasp the full import of what they were saying. Even so, they all four gave an account of themselves, asked in awed tones how he was feeling and whether he was still suffering from the agonies of his torture.

He made no answer, but looked out through the window at the last morsel of daylight, in which a pallid star was already aglimmer.

"How strange," said the poet, also turning to the window, "that we should grow so fond of a presence, even the most

38

remote and unfeeling, as long as it is there without fail at the appointed hour. When I still had my freedom, look you, there at the familiar turning in the lane my heart would leap up on finding the same old inn-sign awaiting me, or the same zigzag crack in the wall . . . No less is happening now with Hesperus here. Hesperus, O friendly star," he declaimed with a surge of irony, waving a hand towards the sky, "those who are about to die salute you!"

At his back the others all raised their eyes towards the star, the young student unwillingly and on the verge of tears.

"I too am afraid," the baron told him. "Though all my life long I have considered myself as being on loan among the living, so that by rights I ought to be the less discomforted. I recall that, when I was in Paris, I made a habit of going of an evening to pay a visit to the ghosts in Place de Grève. There is one belief that I have always held to be irrefutable: that an overwhelming anguish – and what anguish is mightier than a feeling of impending death – saturates the air of a place, stamps itself upon it for ever and ever. Well then, so I used to go to the Place de Grève, and close my eyes and take deep breaths of the air. Instantly a throng of shadows, regicides, murderers, robbers, heretics, aristocrats, rose pressing at my side. I might have counted the wrinkles at the corners of this one's mouth, or made out the hare lip of another; the freckles of a young girl or an old man's ivory brow . . . But, above all, each victim filled my nostrils with the stench of fear and death, our own stench at this moment: the odour of menstruation mixed with urine . . ."

They heard Cirillo shifting on his bunk. Eventually, with great effort, he heaved up his head and shoulders, disclosing the morsel of physiognomy visible through his bandages: a single, piercing pupil and a conceited sneer on swollen lips. Rendered raw by the smarting of his wounds, his voice rang artificial and forced.

"Friends," he said, "kindly reserve such coarseness for your own case. I, who rightly or wrongly bear a pious title, expect my severed head, like the Baptist's on its charger, to exhale an odour of jasmine . . ."

There was in his falsetto such a gratuitously mocking desire to hurt, over and above the mere words which seemed harmless enough, that the baron felt obliged to step across and confront him.

"What do you imply by that? What business have you among us? What right have you to die with us?"

"I am tempted to ask you the same question," returned the other no less sharply. "Who are you, and why are you going to die with me? But it is a given fact that no one chooses either the time or the companions of his death, and, truth to tell, both you and I might have had better luck. The which said, it behoves us to make friends. We have a hatred in common, and that is a bond more depraved even than sharing a common death."

"We both hold the same person in abhorrence," admitted the baron, still on edge, "but not for the same reasons."

"Mine may well be the better," said Cirillo, "but that matters little. Nor do I have any wish to compare them, or to meddle in your affairs. I laugh to scorn your *God the Father*, just as I revere the other, the true Father. I have not opposed this king simply to be a slave to other kings. It was my wish that there should no longer be the high and the low, but that all men should be equal."

The baron was somewhat mollified.

"I have heard speeches galore of this nature, in Brussels, in the Café des Mille Colonnes, among the exiles from Paris. But I venture to wonder if . . ."

Hearing a clamour of voices he broke off and went to the window.

The moon had risen, a small beaked sickle between two

magenta-coloured clouds in which the sunset still lingered. However, it was not on the moon's account that Ingafù had moved; for down below, where the scaffold was nearly erected, he saw the glisten of another sickle and a group of men at work around it, testing the run of the blade in the groove, and whether the command lever released the spring. He did not see, but from a desperate miauling he realized, that as a final experiment someone had forced the neck of a cat into the lunette. He had scarcely time to turn his back before a swish, a thud and a unanimous snort of laughter assured him that all would go smoothly on the morrow.

The soldier shuddered.

"They say the blade is more humane, but speaking for myself, and failing a noble death by ball and powder, I would at least have preferred the noose . . ."

"Bah," retorted Saglimbeni. "Let's be honest, the blade takes but an instant."

"Does it hurt?" asked the student timidly.

For quite some time no one uttered a word. Then the baron spoke.

"Just the same," he said, "these hours must be whiled away. The question is, should it be in talk or in silence?"

"On one occasion," put in Brother Cirillo, "in the Torrearsa castle, I snatched a book from the flames. A licentious work, but blood-curdling at bottom. It was called the *Decameron* . . ."

"You imply," returned the baron, "that if death is a plague we should forget about it by making up stories?"

"Making up stories, no, but some good might come of a confession," said the brigand. "Confessing, I mean, not into the hairy ear of some priest but amongst yourselves."

"What would we gain from it?" asked the soldier.

"Understanding of whether the lives you have lived are

worthily concluded by this stoic death; or whether, on the contrary, it does not sound an untoward false note. But this is altogether your business. I am not one of your company, I am a mere interloper . . ."

Upon this followed an enormous silence. Finally, after long, whispered consultations with the others, it was broken by the baron.

"Give us a subject, then, you who seem so well informed. Even though we don't have a hundred days at our disposal, or a thousand-and-one nights, but just one miserable, short vigil."

Cirillo did not need to be asked twice.

"I am not going to impose limits on you. Let each one tell about himself. For example, when and in what manner, in a scrutiny of his life, he has perchance been happy, or has thought himself to be so, or was thought to be so by others. And what images he will choose from among the shreds and tatters of his days, to keep him company in his mind's eye at the instant when his neck is inserted in the lunette and the cold edge of the blade plunges down to sever it."

"No good for me," objected the soldier. "I don't know much about happiness. If anything I'd tell not a memory at all, but a dream. How every night I enjoy massacring the king in some new fashion: with my nails, with a cobbler's knife, with a peasant's pitchfork . . . This only after he has crawled at my feet and licked the mud off my topboots. And the queen herself come begging and mewling and offering herself naked, and I, with the quip once uttered to a supplicant by her crowned consort, have answered her, 'You will catch cold, madame. Pray get dressed. And do not distress yourself so over a bastard. I will have ten Masses said for his soul . . .'"

"I could have done with you in my gang," sighed the friar.

"You seem right enough too," replied the soldier. "A pity there's no time to get to know each other better. I've always

42

wondered about the extravagances that are told about your life, and how, as the story has it, you married both God and your musket. I'd like it even better if tonight we might receive the sacrament from you instead of from the chaplain ... Though I fear that absolution from a counterfeit friar such as you would not be of much avail to us . . ."

"A poor kind of sacrament indeed," interrupted the baron. "But each of us might speak of what, both for his own sake as for others', may best give understanding or the lie about himself. The alternatives, on this occasion, are few. Let us therefore recount, or else invent, our most memorable hour. Above all I dare to hope that from the telling there might emerge some reason for this destiny of ours, that we might deduce why we are dying and arrive at a hypothesis, at least, regarding that mystery, which the spectacle of the things surrounding us has been; and that we might find some reason for excusing either God or ourselves, before the break of day. For if we do not find this meaning, nor the reason for our dying, then paradoxically I say to you" – and here he addressed the student – "that we would wish to perish come what may, but that you would have the right to tell that name, and to save your skin . . ."

"What, I alone?" Narcissus was horror-struck. "A turncoat like St Peter?"

"Like St Peter," echoed the baron. "Before at dawn we hear the voice of the madman in the dungeons." And he made a feeble effort to imitate a cockcrow.

"So if someone is ready to make a start . . ." suggested the soldier. "Remember that we have only five hours: four for talk, and one for closing our eyes in the silence of our own selves, before that door is opened."

At this with a puff he extinguished the torches, or, where breath did not answer, with his fist, leaving only the wan glimmer of the oil-lamp.

Thereupon, in the semi-dark, the lad spoke up.

"I am the youngest here," he said, "and therefore the most impatient. I think it only right for me to take first turn, and for the rest of you to follow as you think best."

No one objected, and they all huddled together on the student's bed, excepting the friar, who remained on his own.

FIVE

The Student's Tale, or,
Narcissus Saved from the Waters

My story (began Narcissus) will be a love-story. Of how I, denied love from earliest youth, managed to invent it for myself, to take a rib from my side, and with a puff of my breath to give it life and a name. For love, to my way of thinking, is not a fire requiring flint and steel, but a spontaneous combustion of the mind that, only when the flames are already licking and blazing, seeks, outside of itself, a person to take hold on. A transient sentiment endowed with features so opposed to one another as to resemble those diseases referred to by a single name but the symptoms and consequences of which infinitely vary. Into what straits it has led me is, at this moment, plain to everyone: to the brink of perdition. None the less, I cannot bring myself to speak ill of it, since to it I owe – whatever we mean by such a word – my happiness. I will therefore tell of how, from my first youth up, I had tidings of love and desire for it, and hope and disenchantment; of what I did to gain knowledge of it; and of how in the end it gave me full confidence in myself. This, above all else, was its gift. Previously, I was nobody, I had no notion who I was. Only through love did I learn my own lineaments and know myself to be a person.

I begin at the beginning. Mine was a family of wealthy cloth merchants with dealings all over Europe. My father, a despotic and full-blooded man, would return from his long travels to Holland or Turkey, each time with a different woman; whom he insisted on maintaining in the house until he took his departure again with her. My mother, a woman of great beauty, though worn down by his absences and, even more, by those insulting sojourns, clung to him ever more lovingly the more he rejected her. She was capable, in an effort to make him settle, of tempting him with pathetic arts to perform his conjugal duties, in the hope of presenting him, after the one daughter, with the long dreamt-of male heir. I was he, and with my birth I slew her.

My childhood was therefore that of a savage, in a house on the Adriatic, sheer above the sea and begirt at the back by a garden of marvels. In the company of a sister, Olympia, in whose eyes I never ceased to be a culpable matricide; and of an unversed tutor. I saw my father two or three times a year, just time enough for him to appear and vanish again, with women who spoke ever more unfathomable tongues.

I obtained some slight instruction through music, which caught my fancy as I listened in the attic to a musical box that had belonged to my mother, and to the terrific blasts of Caspar the gardener, former trumpeter to a nobleman in the Veneto and chief horn to his hunting parties along the banks of the Brenta. He it was who gave me lessons on the hautbois and the horn, in secret, either in loft or cellar, whence unappreciative ears would not be shattered by our tantivies. Before very long I had no further use for a teacher, and I loved to wander off into the countryside and then, seated in the shade of some tree or wall, to play my instrument at the top of my lungs. Days of enchantment! Nor do I know how many more I might have spent, as like one unto another as they were innocent, had I not one day, while making music in the woods, beheld before me a young peasant girl leading a mare to be mounted. She stopped, and begged me to desist, lest I should frighten the animal. In return she would allow me to keep her company, and to hold the halter. It seemed like a new game to me, so I went. There I saw a noble stallion, fenced in by traves, as they call them, rear up as he caught the scent of the approaching female; and thereafter, aided by hand, plunge himself into the red juices of her, and lose himself upon her. When he withdrew himself from her, the languor of his eyes and of his nostrils were of a melancholy almost human.

I was not there and then all that much discomposed by the novelty of this experience. On the contrary, I acquired from it a kind of childlike pride. Initiated thus into an adult secret, I felt myself bound by the strongest blood-brotherhood, and committed to investigating on my own account by what means the sentiment of love, about which until now I had only heard vaguely, was capable of inciting to such sad and acrobatic practices. Therefore, this being the only way open to me, I began to spy on the copulations of other animals, from dogs to flies, in so far as my prying eyes could ascertain them. Febrile, repellent spasms yet again they seemed to me, and I was discouraged by them. Except when one morning I witnessed two butterflies, kissing wing to wing on a chalice of cornflowers, sweetly succumb.

I had attained, meanwhile, the springtime of my thirteenth year. And more and more often, having laid my brass instrument aside, I would lie propped up against a treetrunk, hands clasped behind my head, and watch my small member swell and rise to the dictates of nature. Nor did I seek for any relief save but to ejaculate dreamlessly that night between the sheets. That notwithstanding, when in Caspar's absence it fell to me one day to milk the goat, a strange feeling came over me as I squeezed her udders. Nor did I scruple on another occasion to attempt to ravish her, not from lust be it said, but from mere curiosity about the mechanics of it. I had no luck, luckily, for the animal leapt away like the shrew she was, leaving me sprawled unbuttoned on the grass.

I thereupon ceased to hear the simple word *love* as a sound of prestige and magic, as were those syllables in Greek which had only to be pronounced to give access to the mysteries. And, in the lays of the poets, I was seized with disgust at anyone who permitted their temples to swell with bovine lust; or else, dazed and besweated, prostrated their satiety beside the body of a stranger-woman.

What should I tell you next? Repudiated by all other objects, I resolved to fall in love with myself, following the example of my namesake, that Narcissus who perished by gazing at his own reflection in a pool. Not infrequently, therefore, my sister would discover me standing naked in front of a mirror, and pummel me with her fists in playful resentment, though not without something strange and troubled in her eyes. For she in the meantime, unlike me, had grown eager for bodily contact. So much so that even my father became aware of it during his fleeting visits, and endeavoured to rein her in by engaging us a tutor. The latter, since my father's homecomings were by now increasingly rare, became our real lord and master. Whence stemmed all my subsequent fortunes.

It happened one day in May. Caspar was weeding the garden while I, as was my wont, all unbeknownst to him, had secluded myself in a nest of leafy branches. I was reading a book, I recall, without really giving it my attention but shutting my eyes and toying with the fatamorganas of sound which I had plucked from it. When I opened them again the serving man had seated himself to rest beneath a brushwood shelter, and was mopping his bare chest with a large blue neckerchief. He was a man of fifty, this Caspar, thickset and sturdy and with a chest like an oak, as befits a horn-player. At that moment Olympia appeared as if from nowhere, fluttering and billowy in her flimsy garments. Now sidling towards the shelter, now retreating from it; just as a bee will hover, in paying court to the intimate parts of a flower. Eventually I saw her slip in beside the man, and ask him some question, and he too astounded to reply. Scarcely a moment later she hoisted up her skirts, and stretched herself out beside him as he sat there. I still retain the vision of that pearl-white belly of hers, with its touch of rotundity, like that of a drowned girl's corpse, where there flowered at the delta of her legs a tuft of hair as fine as a day-old puppy's.

Caspar's face had taken on the colour of a drunkard's – ashen blotched with puce – but his hands remained stonily at his sides. Nor did he stir, either to help or to hinder, when she unbuttoned him. It was at this point that I, in spite of myself, started to yell and thereby parted them.

The outcry brought the tutor to the window. Olympia had not the time, nor perhaps the wish, to readjust her clothing, but accused the gardener of having tried to violate her. In vain I contradicted her.

The result was that the servant was dismissed and that I, whether from pigheadedness or the smart of outraged innocence – or else a sudden urge for adventure – fled along with him. Nor would Caspar have deemed it wise to take me with him, but he could scarcely do other when I, bearing a little bundle of belongings, joined him at the sign of the *Golden Lion*.

I will not linger over the ensuing times. In the company of my comrade I wandered for years from land to land, heedless of the pleasures of youth and stubbornly preserving a remorseless virginity. At the same time, as I grew up and read more deeply, I developed a passion for the freedom of all peoples; which stood for me in the stead of the passion of love. It was at that time, you will remember, that I chanced to fall in with you around a card table and, despite my tender years, you initiated me into the secret mysteries of the Committee. Having aroused the suspicions of the police by the part I had played in sowing the seeds of the "new times" among the students, I was compelled to make my escape to the north, where I arrived with letters addressed by Caspar to his former employer.

This latter was a nobleman of the name of Grimaldi, a person of liberal convictions who owned a Palladian villa at the river's edge; and at its back was a garden the very image of the garden of my childhood. The place at once enraptured me: its ornamental fish-pool adorned with statues, its colonnades and dovecotes, its fruit trees, its shrubberies, its innumerable easeful, sweet, hidden corners. There I regained a peace of mind and a taste for daydreaming which I had allowed to lapse. Hired as a servant, to keep up appearances, I in fact had all the time in the world, and I made good use of it to return to my reading and my youthful enthusiasms; the which I mingled, turn and turn about, with practice on the horn.

This helped towards my promotion, along with other amateur musicians from the neighbouring Villas, to membership of the orchestra assembled in summertime by their lordships, with the object of gladdening the holidays. It was Grimaldi's intention, with their collaboration, to revive one of those nights of fireworks and watermusic which were oftentimes, a century ago, wont to flatter the hearts of kings on the waters of the Thames. A deal of rehearsal was needed for us to learn our parts, but I welcomed the plan, auspicious as the occasion was for casting aside my self-love and turning my fancy to others. It thus came about that, at the appointed hour, my instrument slung over my shoulder, I took up my station on the musicians' barge, which was nothing more than the raft used in the daytime for the transportation of tobacco. With some dozens of us on board, and propelled by slow, rhythmic strokes of the oars, we were to row from villa to villa, following all the meanderings of the river, gathering other craft in our wake until, with unceasing music, we came to our moorings at the "Malcontenta". Here an open-air banquet, preceded by fireworks and followed by a masked ball, was to bring the night's proceedings to a close. And what a night was that! Oh, let me remember it, a comforter to this night I must now endure . . .

There I was in the stern with the brass and the woodwinds, playing with all the spirit and verve in the world; and although perched on the edge of the hard planking, jostled by robust limbs and stentorious lungs, I felt myself to be both postillion and admiral; he who with the merest flourishes of his oliphant guides the oarsmen of love to a fabled Cythera . . . And I glided thus upon the placid waters, into which the oars dipped like fingers into the deeps of a luxuriant head of hair. Between two rival river-banks, this side dark with willow and alder, over there, a-sparkle with lanthorns . . . On I glided and played along with the rest of them, but it was as if I were the only player beneath the upturned vessel of the sky, alone in feeling the sway of the raft and in savouring the bourdon of the current that accompanied our barcarole; alone in observing how the shadows of the oars conspired with the moonbeams to compose the most joyous of alphabets . . .

Some near, some far, the rest of the flotilla followed in our wake, with barges, wherries and skiffs. From time to time they would draw up alongside, the better to harken to our music, perhaps, or to marvel at the sparring of lip or of fingertip that flaunted that flower of sound between the waters and the heavens. Among them all, a wherry more inquisitive and insistent than the rest finally came so close as almost to collide with us. Just then the moon vanished behind a bank of cloud, and a torch promptly lighted in the prow of the wherry illumined as bright as day – between the standing figures of two uniformed officers – the person of a seated girl. I ceased playing and stared at her. Believe me or not, that first glimpse suffices me to tell you now, in all minute particulars, just how she was.

Emerging from her gauzy bonnet I can tell of rich brown hair drawn imperiously taut on either side of a knife-like parting, forming two smooth, soft swaths that broke into ringlets at the temples and cascaded onto her shoulders. A bold and lofty brow, though sadly furrowed by trouble. Her eyes, in contrast, splendoured with all the insouciance of youth, two round doubloons, two drops fallen from a Mediterranean firmament cloudless as yet, nor darkened by the presage of the coming equinox. Finally, in the iris itself, a fickle tricksomeness, matched by another similar; I speak of the lightly parted lips that seemed at every breath to kiss the air. As for her nose, her cheeks, her chin, though a perfection of form and of fusion, they withdrew good-humouredly before that pageant of smiles and glances like modest bystanders before a duel between great heroes. But in no wise did her air and bearing lose their ineffable quality of pride and queenly valour. The which was enhanced by a glitter of gems and the opulence of her gown, spread wide and brushing the plain boards of the deck, though ethereal about the bosom, where the alabaster of her breast, negligently tended by a cashmere shawl, made war upon the moonlight.

All that was missing was knowledge of her name. But at that moment, from beneath the awning of a nearby vessel, came a hail of "Eulalie!" And she turned; and so I discovered who it was I loved. She laughed, too, as she called back "What now?" With the result that I, glimpsing that little minnow of a tongue flickering between her teeth, knew I would have died a thousand deaths merely to catch it in my net.

At this moment I forgot all else; and it needed no more to cause me to tumble headlong into the river, along with my instrument.

So gentle was the splash that not a soul noticed. However,

when my opening fanfare in the Minuet was nowhere to be heard, they looked vainly for me at my post, and pandemonium ensued. But already rescuing hands had hoisted me aboard the vessel that my lass was in . . .

"Narcissus saved from the waters!" she teased me remorselessly when I stammered out my name, streaming water onto her feet from every inch of my body.

The two officers of the escort, who were in fact only masquerading as such, helped me to thaw out the marrow of my bones with a gulp or two of raw liquor. Shortly afterwards we landed, and I was able better to fortify myself in the kitchen of the villa where, for a change of clothing, I was given the freedom of a cupboard full of fancy-dress costumes. For some reason I chose a Mephisto cap to top off a Harlequin costume, and then bided my time until the trays of victuals had been cleared from the lawns, and the firework display had begun, before launching myself, unsuspected by the guests, in pursuit of Eulalie. I had no trouble in recognizing her, though she had masked her eyes with a black velvet domino. More difficult, when dancing began, to obtain her as my partner for a waltz . . . She appeared not to recognize me, and nor did I desire it. I was content to circle the floor with her and to hold her in my arms. I was in love, I was in bliss . . .

I have oftentimes since then thought back upon that hosanna flash that was my love for Eulalie. And I have come to the conclusion that it was as we read in the doctrines of that sage of antiquity, which my tutor strove to teach me when I was a lad; according to which we preserve in our souls the model of an Idea beheld already in another life and, in our new state, lost to us. Until on this earth we chance to meet with incarnate examples of it, and in these the recollection of that Idea of a sudden enflames the mind, turning it from beast into philosopher.

53

Such a thing, that evening, was Eulalie: Idea of beauty and of soul, a triumph of flame and of flesh, celestial body descended into the world of sense, and sense itself transported beyond the reach of the senses . . . Something that, as far as I can understand them, might better be elucidated by two words: magnetism, electricity.

I was therefore on wings as I held her in my arms, offering not a single word, but at the same time visibly shivering from head to foot. When, later, a gentleman approached and asked her for the pleasure, she proceeded to tease me with, "Saved from the waters well you may be, but from catching cold, not a chance!"

I perceived that she had seen through my disguise, as I through hers, and this created a complicity between us. Especially when, as she was whirled off by her new partner, she doffed her mask with a swift gesture and shed upon me a smile like a sunbeam. I could think of nothing but to reply in kind, removing my own mask and revealing to her, but also to the world at large, the features of a servant, an intruder. Would I had never done it! Grimaldi had to intervene and hustle me away by the arm amidst a murmur of universal disapproval. Having doffed the Doges' horned headgear which served him as disguise, he delivered a fatherly reprimand for this imprudent performance.

I took no heed of this, but urged him to tell me about Eulalie, and who she was. I was aghast to hear that she was already wedded, to a certain Veniero Manin, an aristocrat now languishing in prison in the Piombi in Venice, having admitted to being master of a Carbonari lodge.

"What!" I cried. "And what of me?" Thus firmly and childishly had I persuaded myself, since I so passionately felt I belonged to her, that she was mine.

I can scarcely tell of what storms raged in my heart and vitals over the next few days. My conscience tortured also by the thought of that absentee: hard indeed to forgive myself for laying siege to his wife while he was in durance vile for my very own Cause. In vain did Grimaldi attempt to cheer me up. Over and over I cried out, "I am lost!" and wished to lie down and die.

I was in such straits as these when she sent a courier to summon me. The letter came from the Lagoon, whither she had gone to be the nearer to her husband. I read over the few lines, and neither hesitated nor thought twice about the duty which lay before me. For I was in love, as one is at nineteen, and in Italy.

I bade farewell to my patron, took a brace of pistols and a modicum of baggage, and set forth. It was a short journey, but no safer for that. Until then I had been at the Villa, unharassed, among discreet, well-affected neighbours, posing as an innocent. The highway now presented not a few perils. My description, my notoriety as a bandit and the price on my head were on every tongue. Although I was an outsider, and indeed for that very reason, I was bound to be the object of inquisitive gossip. More than likely the imperial police would reap the reward where the king's men had failed . . . By the grace of God I won through. But it was not fear that caused my heart to thump at every step as I climbed the stairs.

Finally I knocked, the door opened. It was the first time since the ball that I had been in her presence, and more than ever it astonished me that she did not cry out that she loved me, so natural a thing was loving her for me. She told me, instead, that she knew of my prowess, of my revolutionary escapades, and that this was why she had sent for me, deeming no one more worthy to be at her side in a fearful undertaking, which was no less than her husband's escape from prison.

"So tenderly does she love him," I thought, and a lump came into my throat. "She will never love me, how can she ever love me?"

Nevertheless I fell on one knee and declared: "I have always been of a mind to accept challenges from which I might emerge the loser. This one, in addition, I am bound to lose whatever may be the outcome; and I well know why. Be that as it may, I lay at your feet my strength, my life, my hopes. Do with them as you will."

Impetuously she bent and kissed me on the brow.

"Your life will not be at stake," she said. "At least, such is my hope. My plan is to visit my husband in his cell, as is permitted me on certain established days, accompanied by a sister of his who in age and build somewhat resembles him. Then, when they have exchanged clothing, for the two of us to gain freedom, leaving to the plucky girl the discomforts of a trifling sentence while rescuing my husband from an implacable condemnation."

As I expressed doubts concerning the success of the enterprise, "Have no fear," she reassured me. "The evening shadows will conspire with me to blind the eyes of the guards. But even more effective will be a well-filled purse."

In the meanwhile she had raised me to my feet with an affectionate hand. "Your task," she proceeded, "will be outside the walls, providing carriages, fresh horses, weapons and clothing; and thereafter to escort us over the Apennines to the retreats of *God the Father*, with which you are already familiar . . ."

I gave my acquiescence without fully comprehending her, for I was in a trance, seeing her there , vibrant beside me, her cheeks a glow of coral-red, not from shame, but fervour.

Thereafter we met daily. I begged her, respectfully, and claiming nothing in return, whether I might not speak to her a little of love. Much as one makes one's confession to a grille in a confessional, or to a star.

A solace that was granted me on condition that I asked for not a single syllable in reply. And thus it came to pass at every meeting, at the hour appointed for me to take my leave. Even today I smile at it, thinking of the bizarre procedure at these trysts of ours, subject for hour after hour to the most icy reasonings, to the scrutiny of our schemes for the escape, that it might not be impeded by the least erroneous calculation or freak of chance, concluding then with a soliloquy, a rapture on my part. And she impassively listening, with not a stirring of visage or of body to induce me to hope that she shared my feelings. Until, the sand-glass having been twice turned over, which was the limit granted me by her patience, she would rise from her invisible throne and offer me her hand; and with the seal of a philanthropic kiss, dismiss me.

Came the day for the escape. As to the success of it, all Europe told the tale and I need add no more. What you are not sufficiently acquainted with are the incidents which befell us on our journey, when we left the territories of the Empire and entered those of the Papal States. We had arrived there in travelling costume with fresh horses fit to cross the mountains. Already (and I know not whether in fairness of judgement or in a fit of jealous envy) I had come to look upon Veniero as a weak man, fatuous both in feature and in manner. Two things were a mystery to me: how he had dared to espouse the cause of the people, thereby exposing himself to the thunderbolts of governments; and how on earth he could have aroused affection in a heart so proud and tender as was hers . . .

We rode by night, choosing the most out-of-the-way routes in order to avoid the papal gendarmerie, but ever and anon obliged to seek food and the relief of sleep in some lonesome hostelry. And so it happened, when we were already past the worst straits, and were consuming a repast in the taproom of an inn, that in there came three persons with the air of hunters about them, with haversacks, telescopes and carbines, the latter slung slantwise across their backs. They enquired of us who we were and where we were bound for, in all good faith and just chatting around the board. At which Veniero panicked, and for no reason at all produced his documents, forged in the name of one of the Savelli family and procured for him in Rome by the great Vanina, famous in Carbonari circles some years previously, but now the wife of an eminent prince.

On seeing these papers, the eldest of the men gave a start, then spoke aside to the others. After which he bade us farewell, averring that he must hasten to the boar-shooting butts. We caught his meaning better when he returned with a troop of gendarmes, charging us with the fact that the young man whose name appeared on the passport had, as was common knowledge, been dead for a year.

But Eulalie, bold as brass: "Quite so," she said, "but the fact is that we are travelling incognito. We are lovers, and eloping. We are loath that our true names should leak out."

And with this she whispered into the sergeant's ear the name of a Prince of the Church which caused him to blanch.

"What about *him*?" objected the soldier, stabbing a finger at me.

"He is in our service," replied the woman, regally.

Such brazen excuses might well have satisfied the man, had not the leader of the hunting party butted in.

"There's a search out, I know, for a prisoner escaped from the Piombi. There's a price on his head and I want it. A better morning's bag, I say, than any wild boar!"

I held my tongue, my hands on the butts of my pistols. But Veniero suddenly spoke up.

"What's the use of protecting him?" he ejaculated coldly. And pointing to me: "There is the man you want, Veniero Manin."

Eulalie cast him a look of inexpressible horror, and I one of stupefaction. But with magnanimity I replied, "It's the truth, I am he! Take me if you can!" And so saying I made to draw my pistols, but they were already upon me. In the ensuing turmoil Veniero made his escape, but *she* remained. At that precise instant, from the merest flicker of an eyelid, I knew that I was loved.

Some time later, in Rome, in a cell in Castel Sant'Angelo, awaiting the extradition requested by our government, I received from her the demonstrations of a passion which at long last was the rival of my own. She came to visit me daily, she being free as air, having been accused only of the mildest malfeasances, from which the friendship of Princess Savelli had rapidly absolved her. And she would speak to me through the grating, hungrily rubbing her lips against the iron that barred them from mine. Ah, how many burning words and dreams of freedom and vows of voluptuousness, which left me for dead, unable to rise from the bench on which I sat and listened . . .

Eventually, three years ago almost to the day, came the word for me to be extradited. At night, without warning. But well you knew the time and place, my friends, by secret advisement from *God the Father*, who truly never better than then envisioned, predicted and acted from his exalted seat. Ah, what wouldn't the Governor himself give to know what a personage is masked behind that nickname!

The assault on the guard escorting me to the royal prisons, well, you accomplished that yourselves; I knew little of it, being manacled in the dark between the four walls of the vehicle, my back to the horses so that I should not know where we were going. But I have in my mind's eye a memory, that as soon as my foot touched the ground, and you had unchained me, and we had embraced one another at last, we all of us raised our faces in token of gratitude to the beauteous vault of heaven. Though almost on the instant I felt a stab at the heart as, in the grass, I trod unwittingly on the corpse of a foe, a beardless corporal from Fondi with whom I had been cracking jokes during the journey, and who now yielded beneath my feet with all the pliant, disjointed inertia of the newly slain. This was driven from my mind by Eulalie, who had accompanied you, and was waiting behind a tree, on tenterhooks to greet me . . .

And thus it was, that night, when we had at last reached safety, that truly I learnt from her of what love is. You, friends, were asleep in the shelter of a barn, we in a dell beneath the naked sky, overarched by branches broad as a church dome. And this, in your eyes, might appear too shameless, but I cannot refrain from putting into words the relishes then revealed to me, as shyly she disrobed herself in such faint light as filtered through to us, and which was not moonlight, no, but a foretoken of it, a luminescence, an efflorescence, such as clings to a hedge when a firefly has passed. Herself then, white and a-tremble above me, scarcely more versed than I was in the rhythms of love. And how, together, we drowned in a vortex of motion. Waves flowing through me from head to heel, all but imperceptible at first, like the whorls of an undertow; then more turbulent, as if urged by a sudden breeze, and then rollers that crashed within me like the rush of white horses in a storm; but in a trice becalmed, while in the conch of my ear sounded the notes of oboes from my long-past summer afternoons . . .

"Eulalie," mutely I cried, and with tireless fingers stroked her cheek, fumbled for a ringlet to twine them in, for another grape-like cluster of her body to mouth and to sip at . . . And the moon came to my aid, as it had that night on the river, as supine I lay, drinking in the glory of her countenance poised above me.

On every side such silence, and such peace . . .

*

So be it. Since then I have had other loves; at other times, and more so, I have been astonished at the plenitude of my bliss. But that night only, and no other, shall I picture in my mind four hours hence, as the blade's edge bites in.

SIX

Interlude of
Thunder and Lightning

"A diverting little tale," was Saglimbeni's comment, "but the ending is rotten. You might have spared us that funereal conclusion."

"Mark the innocent!" snapped back Cirillo. "As if we needed a town crier to keep us reminded of death, when it's graven on our hearts every moment."

Then spoke Ingafù, and "Thank you, Narcissus," he said, "for reminding us of love, and of music, and of moonlight, and sounding in our ears the celestial tinkles of youth . . . Though it may be that some of us, in those last moments, will be pondering on weightier matters."

"You really think so!" cried Saglimbeni. "Well, it may be the effect of what they call deathbed euphoria, but I must admit to having contrived a little piece of nonsense on the subject of last wishes, a wish for each of the five senses, with the addition of a sixth, as frivolous as you please. With a dedication to the Governor, too, should he make a plea for it tomorrow morning. But also to all of you, if you are willing to hear it."

"Please yourself," they muttered without enthusiasm, while he, making a point of turning towards Narcissus, for clearly he was eager to amuse him, or at least was generous enough to try and distract him, began as follows:

Now while I am yet alive
Of last wishes I have five:
For my last savour of the earth
Give me a wine of noble birth;
For my last touch I would prefer
To sink my fingers in kitten-fur;
To fill my ears, this is my choice:
To hear the wide sea's mighty voice;
For my last sight before I die
I crave an amethyst-coloured sky;
For scent, I ask to plunge my nose
Into the dewy heart of a rose.
Lastly I would like to mix
With these five, a number six:
Dearly would I like to have,
Before I face the slaughter,
— Pressed into my arms in love —
The headsman's daughter!

"Your squibs used to be a darned sight more mordant," the soldier broke in with a wry face. The others, too, remained perfectly serious, and Narcissus was alone in granting his friend a half-smile.

"As far as sound goes," he said, "your wishes are fulfilled tonight. The sea is at your service."

And true it was that there at the foot of the island, where it fell sheer down to the waves, rose now and again a tumultuous roar upon the rocks, almost an animal cry, as from some sudden warfare of the winds.

"Whom shall we turn to next for a story?" enquired the baron, to dispel the embarrassment of the moment. But Agesilaos had an objection to raise.

"What's all the hurry? There's time and to spare. We'll wait until the second watch comes round."

He thrust his head into the embrasure of the window and looked about. Especially at the sky where the stars were now overcast, though there was still a trace of that slip of a moon. At his back, the others lay in silence. It may be that some one of them, despite the general agreement, had dozed off; or someone perhaps, heavy hearted, was hanging on the brink of sleep.

Until, after a minute or two, Narcissus spoke at random to his companions in the dark:

"Asleep? Are you all sleeping? Ah! Impossible for me! A terrible thought has come to me, and I must unbosom myself. It is this: that if I were to hammer at that door, and cry out for a last hearing, and ram the name that's scalding my tongue down the Governor's throat . . ."

"You'll never do it!" interposed the baron. "Otherwise you would not just have said it, you would have done it."

"Notions born of the night-time," pontificated the friar to excuse the lad. "In the womb of the dark one feels safe from prying eyes and up to daring the darkest of misdeeds. I recall a particular scoundrel amongst all the blackguards in my gang, who, whenever he lay down beside me in the innermost recesses of our lair, and heard me saying the Lord's Prayer before going to sleep, as indeed I have done all my life, would yell 'Up yours!' and stab two vulgar fingers aimed at God.

"Or at least this was his story, for indeed I couldn't see him. But he would never have done that by daylight! At any rate, he gave it up when I informed him of that oriental proverb, which states that a black ant on a black table on a pitch-black night can be seen by no one . . . except by God."

"May I tell you another of my poisonous thoughts?" persisted the lad. "Escape! I've been tormenting myself about it these last few days. Impossible, you've always maintained, and so be it. But that he, our own *God the Father*, has never sent us a signal, never rapped a flake of plaster from our walls

. . . that he claims our loyalty as his right, and calmly accepts the sacrifice of our lives . . ."

Again the friar broke in.

"I have no wish to set myself up as a tactless judge of the afflictions of others," he said, "but speaking in parables and similitudes, as was my way at one time when haranguing the troops after sacking a place, I tell you that even Christ on the Mount of Olives waited in vain for a sign from the Father, and feared himself forsaken . . . Come now, do you imagine that a burlesque *God the Father* is more worthy, and honour-bound to answer you, when the true, Eternal Father did not answer His own Son?"

"Don't bring religion into it," chided the soldier. "You and your Eternal Fathers and eternal paternosters! The truth is that, what with the sea being so rough and the garrison so strong, this rock is impregnable. Furthermore, if to save our skins he were to suspend the Grand Design, on those terms I wouldn't dream of it . . ."

Brother Cirillo gave a start but said not a word. Instead, it was the student who spoke.

"All the same, if we bribed someone here . . . Eulalie did it, even for a husband she didn't love."

"He who was actually able to walk out disguised as a woman!" rejoined Agesilaos with a mocking edge to his voice. "They must have had moles on guard at the Piombi, not sentries!"

"It is not as unbelievable as you may think," put in the baron. "The very same method was employed by the Comte de Lavallette at the Conciergerie, to escape from the clutches of Louis XVIII. And as for a man pretending to be a woman, or vice versa, leaving aside the case of the Chevalier d'Éon, which is common knowledge, I would like to recount to you an anecdote which was doing the rounds of Paris at the time when I resided there, and which is to the point . . . It concerns a student recently arrived in Paris from the Americas and introduced into a literary circle, prominent in which was a person who went by the name of George, but was in reality a woman writer who, in order to avoid the vexing servitude of her sex, made a habit of attiring herself in masculine clothing. Introduced into her society, the student was asked by her whether her writings were much read in America.

"A great deal sir," he replied, "and they are most highly spoken of. However . . ."

"Pray continue. You may speak freely."

"You are criticized," said the young man blushingly, "for being overfond of changing costume and sometimes dressing up as a woman . . ."

His listeners were still laughing, or at least smiling, when the baron suddenly rose to his feet and started pacing nervously up and down the gangway between the bunks. Something untoward must have shaken him, something of which he himself was but dimly aware. He crossed to the window, sniffed the outside air with wide flaring nostrils, peered up at the swift clouds scurrying across the sky, and shuddered. In a moment or two he was himself again, taken up with other thoughts, like a hound that has lost the scent.

"To return to our former discourse," he resumed, "*God the Father* is not able to do whatever he pleases. Deprived of ourselves, who spoke and acted for him, while he was unknown to the other members of the fellowship, and prudent of very necessity, what can you expect of him?"

"If that be so," – Agesilaos returned to the question – "what will become of the Grand design?"

"It will be carried through," replied the baron. "And precisely in virtue of our deaths. For by dying without betraying it we shall render the Cause sacred in the eyes of the people. Led as lambs to the slaughter, apostles of his word even unto death: thus will they speak of us tomorrow, as they do already

66

on country market days and in the squares of the capital. The year will not see its end before, from the very gutters, with *God the Father* at their head, the People will arise . . ."

"This," said the friar, "is a matter which you will do better to mull over this time tomorrow night, with the fish at the bottom of the sea." And he applauded derisively.

Then, gravely, he added, "Sublime words, Ingafù, but somewhat low on salt and long on nonsense. You are not mean in years, but I am your senior. Ah, how many hotheads have I seen fall because they had deluded themselves that they could take a rabble and make a people of it . . . Blind banner-bearers who promise the sun, moon and stars, of whom I say 'Give them a wide berth.'"

"We, on the contrary," declared the baron proudly, "claim that a handful of men prepared to die with their boots on are capable of leading the many to insurrection."

"Well said!" exclaimed Saglimbeni. "It's the same idea as that Aria of Donizetti's." And before anyone could stop him he had begun softly to sing:

> *Il palco è a noi trionfo*
> *ove ascendiam ridenti,*
> *ma il sangue dei valenti*
> *perduto non sarà.*
> *Avrem seguaci a noi*
> *più fortunati eroi,*
> *ma s'anco avverso ed empio*
> *il fato a lor sarà,*
> *avran da noi l'esempio*
> *come a morir si va . . .**

* Triumph for us is the scaffold which laughing we ascend, but the blood of the valiant shall not go to waste. We shall have our followers, heroes more fortunate; but even if destiny to them should be unjust and hostile, from us they may take example of how men go to die . . .

"Pipe dreams," resumed Brother Cirillo, "like those of a man who fancies everything larger than life, and judges a mere shadow to be a solid body."

"Call them pipe dreams if you like," retorted Ingafù. "But I know that people remain cold and indifferent unless they are warmed by the blood of martyrs. You must dig your kitchen garden if you want fat snails."

"Come now, gentlemen," broke in the poet. "This is no time for bickering. Whoever is in the right will only be so for the scanty few hours that are left to us. In the meanwhile, baron, without asking you to play the soothsayer and sibyl, but inasmuch as you are in a position to know, and to confide in us, pray satisfy this curiosity of mine: how much longer has our well-beloved sovereign got to live?"

"Just a little longer than us," – and Ingafù's voice seemed laden with suppressed exultation – "but a little less than the Governor . . ."

"Which means that he's only got a month or two," they all chuckled, with the exception of Brother Cirillo.

"Very well," said the latter pensively. "I gather, then, that even though by the skin of his teeth he survived your attempt on his life on Jubilee day, he will certainly not survive the next attempt, and that to go to the devil he will in no wise be short of chances; whether shot in his box at the Opera, or poisoned with *acqua Tofana* at his birthday banquet, or stabbed at the Review, sooner or later . . . What a pity that neither you nor I will see that day!"

"And that day, when will it be?" asked Agesilaos. But the baron made no reply.

"Who will give me his oath," said Narcissus, "that at least when the tyrant is dead the world will be a happier place?"

"Now there's a sensible question!" exclaimed the friar. And in his wake: "It commonly happens," said Saglimbeni, "that a tyrant is succeeded by a son who excels him in evil. But ours is a childless king, which is a blessing. Once he is dead . . ."

"With his successor matters will improve," said Brother Cirillo ironically. "His heir is the younger brother, and you all know what *he* is like. There are so many tales of his licentiousness, although he can't spit out two words together to a woman. He's a gambler as well, so they say . . ."

Swifter than the shadow of a passing wing, a smile flitted across the faces of the four men.

"You used to be an *habitué* of the theatre," said the baron, turning to the poet. "So tell me, what's the name of that piece of De Musset's, with a Medici prince who had a cowardly cousin?"

Saglimbeni gave a slight shake of the head, though it was unclear whether he meant he was ignorant in the matter, or merely that he had no wish to pursue the subject.

The soldier picked up the invitation, and wandered off at his own sweet will.

"I don't expect a republic," he said. "'Republic' is too big a word, and to the common people has an ugly ring to it. Likewise, they are repelled by 'equality'. They would rather remain abject and grovel in the mud for largesse scattered from a palace balcony. All the same, this king of ours is not only cruel but miserly, and by now they've had enough of him. Sated with him and starving for bread . . . From these two excesses the new people will be born."

"Every insurrection starts from a surfeit and a hunger," agreed the baron. "So much the better if both are present."

"Oh, how I wish this night had no tomorrow!" moaned Narcissus out of the blue.

"The chances are against you," replied Saglimbeni. "It is highly unlikely that day fails to follow night . . ."

He did not finish. His words were drowned by an impromptu crash. An explosion had taken place in a sky which previously had been so clear. Rapidly the moon vanished, routed by a rain-cloud, while in its stead innumerable flashes bloomed forth the pallor of lilies, striking into the cell and flooding the faces of the five men with a visionary lustre. Each face more wild-eyed and dumbstruck than the last, as to their ears arose the alarm of the sea which, lashed by the tail of a dragon, oh! how cruelly did it rage upon the reefs of the island.

The first gust of wind had blown out the solitary lamp, and "the baron!" was the first thought and cry of all as, in the pitchy black, they heard a human bellow issue from his direction, then the thud of a body on the floor, and the sounds that bear witness to one who is rolling and writhing in agony. At which they hastened to his aid with all speed, groping wildly towards the moaning sounds, while Narcissus rushed to the door to cry for help. Picked out by the beam of the lanthorn thus produced, Agesilaos was seen to bend over the man, take him up in his arms, caress his wrinkled face, his remaining grey hairs – an Aeneas.

It took some time for Ingafù to regain his senses, for the tempest was still raging, while the sea, thrashed by the wind, ceased not its groanings. But thunder and lightning had to cease altogether, and the weather as seen through the little window to appear less threatening, before the old man regained his customary strength of mind and authority. With a wave of the hand he dismissed the warder who, armed with the lanthorn, had remained at the peephole to spy on this untoward disturbance. Then, overcoming the slight tremor which still affected his speech, he began with false heartiness:

"How strange it is to be ever afflicted by this panic fear of cloudbursts, as if I still had aught to fear from the heavens. It was born in me many years ago, and I have never disclosed its cause. This is a propitious time for me to render account of it, especially to myself. Therefore, let me claim as mine the second place in our series of narratives."

They all clustered round him, obedient, attentive. He with his years, and the discretion of his years, had long since dominated them; he who had picked out each one, and had enabled them to mount ever closer to the enigma which was their Leader. And more than one of them owed him his life; albeit, on this occasion, his death.

"This tale of mine, my friends," announced Ingafù, "is without a title." And the others kept silent while he told the following story.

SEVEN

The Baron's Tale

I had scarcely reached the years of my majority, but from one day to the next I realized that I could no longer perform an action, or pronounce a phrase, but that within it, like the canker in the rose, there lurked, if I may so express myself, a certain proviso of the mind. I would be caressing a woman, and all the time thinking, "What will come of this?" If complimented on the cut of a frock-coat, or the finesse of a witticism, I would smile, I would blush . . . Though not without a spasm of irritation, a kind of insurrection of the nerves, an infinitesimal shudder of the mind, which never rose to the level of consciousness, but tended merely to congeal into sluggish fragments of self-doubt, such as "But really I . . ." "However, if . . ." "Yes, but . . ."

This was the very poison of my youth, from which I recovered only late in life. True, I possessed the most coveted gifts: health, wealth, good looks . . . None the less, coming home in the evening, whether from some frivolity at court, or from a day's shooting, I could never blow out my lamp and give myself up to peaceful slumber, but hour after hour I would stare wide-eyed into the darkness and there, as if written on a slate, I would read overwhelming nothingness . . .

I know not if it will help you to fathom the root of my affliction, but I should add that that was the time of the *cholera morbus*, when so many of my fellows, hale and hearty,

I saw perish daily; and everything treated as filth, even the letters I received from abroad, secured with twine, were subject to quarantine just as people were. This may have given a certain sombreness to my cast of thought. Or it may have been the moral fables of that little count from the Marches, banned by the censors, but slipped me under the counter by the bookseller Starita; and which I read, at first reluctantly, but later with deadly profit. Indubitably day by day I was swiftly aging, with a sense of mindless and perpetual vacuity, wishing myself neither good nor ill, nor turning my head if someone cried my name in the street. I had become nobody, with no wish to take part in life, and a stranger twice over; that is, both in the eyes of others, and in my own.

The clean contrary was Secundus, my twin brother. He was called Secundus on account of having emerged half an hour later than I from our mother's womb; but he had accepted his misfortune in good part. He was content with little: books from France, a few amorous diversions, the game of chess . . . And always with that air of equanimity, that angelic love of truth and justice, and assurance that the miseries of the many were shortly to be remedied by the efforts of the few.

These seemed to me rash aspirations, and I did not fail to exhort him to caution. He paid me no heed. Letters from Fabrizi in Spain fell into the hands of a censor, his name was mentioned in them, and he barely had time to flee into France.

This did not mean that I lost the friendship of the notables of the kingdom; on the contrary, they flocked around me much concerned, and condoled with me as over the tragedy of a kinsman who had gone out of his mind. But I wrapped myself up all the more in my sluggish torpors, through which intermittently ran the feeling that it were better to die than to repeat myself, identical and futile, every morning in the mirror.

The harmless, absurd frivolities I then threw myself into, with the sole aim of distinguishing myself from the common run of people, and putting new blood into the hollow carcass that was me, earned me the repute of an eccentric, but only very fleeting relief. At this point I resolved to travel.

On the eve of my departure, I remember, going as the custom is to take leave of the king, on the staircase I met *God the Father*; though I did not, of course, suspect his secret identity, and that he was the invisible motive power behind all sectarian intrigues.

"That hothead brother of yours," he said to me haltingly, feigning to trip over his words, not from a defect of speech, but because of that peculiar manner of his, which you are all familiar with, of holding a listener's attention by leaving him hanging between apprehension and amazement, uncertain as to the sequel to the suspended word. "If you meet him in Paris," he continued, still straining for each syllable, "tell him from me to come back home, prostrate himself before his sovereign, and obtain his clemency. Men of his stamp are more useful here than at the *Café de la Régence* . . ."

He was, as I suppose – and not without a touch of contempt – alluding to my brother's addiction to the game of chess, of which that café was a public and illustrious arena. I replied rather wanly that I would certainly pass on the message; but in fact I bundled it away with similar things heard from others at other times. In any case, I felt divorced from all commitments, and in the grip of an all-consuming passion, which was to discover for myself, at last, a face, a name, a meaning.

During the preparations for my travels, in fact, I had been falling more and more under the spell of my malady. So much so, that my previous affliction, that of observing myself intolerably identical in every mirror in my room, was superseded – can you imagine? – by the horror of sometimes not seeing myself there at all; of no longer seeing my own person in the glass, but in its place the reflection of the walls and the furniture behind me. As if at this point I were nothing but air and transparency, and had lost not only my shadow, like Peter in the fairy-tale, but the very substance of my body.

The groundless fears of a saturnine cast of mind, I can but suppose; but which I take the liberty of recounting to you so that you may understand what precipice I was on the brink of.

I set off at last, with a single servant and scant baggage, on a tour of Europe. For a year I avoided Paris, not wishing to show myself to Secundus in all the wretchedness of my present condition. I did not even take the trouble to send him a courier bearing *God the Father*'s message; for, not knowing the true identity of the sender, I had not grasped its hidden meaning. But in the end, after Vienna and London, Geneva and Lyons, I set foot on the banks of the Seine, and there took lodgings in a small apartment at Les Batignolles, simply furnished and far from the bustle of the centre.

The city was still ringing with outcry over the nineteen victims of the Boulevard du Temple and the arrest of Fieschi. This earned me a triple mistrust, of my landlord, the neighbours, and the local gendarmerie: all alarmed by my foreign appearance. But I, in my black frock-coat, rode with unseeing solemnity over their aversions, of which I learnt only later, when the evident innocence of my demeanour had disarmed them.

Meanwhile I took to touring the city, but without any love of it. Places and men alike, the more they are packed with history the less I warm to them. I am fondest of towns with not much of a past, tucked away in some fold of the plain, with a single bell-tower and a public garden.

True to myself, in the capital I had singled out a small garden outside the gates, as simple as I could have desired it, and there I would go with the *Journal des Débats* under my arm, to enjoy the fresh air along with a few old women armed with parasols.

Here, peacefully, I would read, every now and then imperceptibly raising my eyes to the bench opposite, where a lone girl, of similar persuasions, came every day to sit in the shade of a plaster statue of Pomona.

Lovely she was; and she returned my glance, inserting her finger between the pages to keep her place. With her blond hair falling loose onto the salience of her bosom, and an amiable pout on her lips. I never spoke to her, although she seemed to desire it, to be waiting for it. Once it happened that I retrieved her straw hat, which the wind had robbed her of and carried like a go-between to my feet; but I restored it to her with a slight bow, and in silence.

Subsequently I regretted this, and felt a dull self-pity. "Here I am as dead as mutton," I thought to myself. "And yet I am still in my youth!"

At which my thoughts turned to Secundus, whose impulsiveness and warm-hearted lust for life I knew well. He lived at not a little distance, on the island in the middle of the river; and I, far from seeking him out, had not even given him news of myself and my arrival in town. No ill-will intended, but in virtue of a composite emotion, a mingling of fear and absent-mindedness. However, as I thus idled away my time, with the pages of a newspaper spread on my knee, and running through the possible reasons which caused me to shun him, a sudden thought burst on me: that he, Secundus, was in all innocence to blame for my misfortunes; that I, the first born, at the price of secret remorse and self-annihilation was expiating the crime of having deprived him of the rights of primogeniture.

"By half an hour," I said out loud, causing the girl opposite to give a start. "Just a miserable half-hour's advantage!"

I leapt to my feet and ran off, leaving the girl dumbfounded. For it had dawned on me that, in order to achieve a cure, I had only to share everything with my brother, to give him half my titles and possessions; and in exchange to ask of him half his noble illusions. Only in this manner could I reassemble and rebaptize the single individual who was the two of us.

I therefore sought out Secundus and was received with warmth and many an embrace. He introduced me into his circle of friends. When I intimated to him my intention of sharing our inheritance he refused with vehemence.

"What nonsense is this, and what mess of potage are you offering me?" said he. "And in any case it is not certain that the seniority belongs to you. More than one savant maintains that he who is second to see the light was first to be conceived. And I am that one."

He mistook my surprise for misgiving, so "Be of good cheer," he added quickly. "Nothing is changed. My coat of arms is freedom."

We were at Procopio's, and with us were a crowd of young men wearing their black hair long and clustered round an old man whose white locks protruded from beneath his silk cap.

"Equality before liberty," proclaimed the latter, thumping the floor with his stick; and I was told he was the celebrated Buonarroti. "We cannot be free if we are not equal!"

'Equal, certainly," replied Secundus gently, "but first, free."

Whereupon a quarrel broke out between them, eventually dominated by the old man's voice.

"There are many fanatics," he said, "with the words freedom and republic forever on their lips, but only to use them to establish a new and yet worse aristocracy on the ruins of the old."

Secundus flushed scarlet.

"There are many," he retorted, "who sow discord between the classes, instead of fostering unity between them. And they claim that the deliverance of the people is advantaged by the usurpation of the rights of others."

And thus they carried on for a space, with the names of Saint-Simon and Mazzini, Robespierre and Babeuf upon their lips, hurling them at one another like stones from a sling while I, alone in my corner, likened them to children, too absorbed in their game to notice that a malignant old man is spying on them. Although the white-haired Buonarroti seemed the most childish of them all, while the grown-up spy's part was my own.

Later, alone with Secundus, I learnt many things: that he had vowed himself to the emancipation of the world; and that he would return home, as was asked of him in the message I had brought him, now that the time for action was imminent. When I inquired what led him to think so, he leant close to my ear.

"I am held to the most ferocious silence," he whispered, though there was no one within earshot. "But to you, my own brother, I am bound to speak. You have brought me no mere counsel, but an order. He who entrusted it to you in our homeland is the leader of us all. He is no out-of-touch Genoese refugee lecturing us from London. No, he speaks from the very heart of the enemy court."

And with this he spoke a name into my ear.

In such a way did I learn of the wellnigh incredible identity of that person, and of the consequent plans for insurrection. But none the less I remained stony, despairing of bringing my brother to my way of thinking; my brother for whom I felt such strong bonds of blood, but a diversity and remoteness of feeling.

In the end I resolved to reveal to him the whole truth about my state of mind. He heard me out with astonishment; then he smiled.

"I do not know which of us is the elder," he said. "But

there is no doubt that you have less savvy. That non-being and absence which you speak of do not arise from here," and he touched his breast, "but from here." He tapped his finger against his brow. "You have not yet understood the times you live in, just as you do not understand this city, which carries the flag for them throughout the world."

We were in a belvedere in the vicinity of Père-Lachaise, where he had taken me to show me at first hand the scene of a recent novel, and we viewed the whole city spread below us.

"Look at her!" he exclaimed. "She's seething like a cauldron. Listen to the bubbling of her, up from the banks of the river, from the hovels and the palaces and the workshops. Like a rock-dammed torrent, like a grenade about to detonate. Does she not lie there, on the banks of the Seine, like a sleeping colossus? Of which, over here, you perceive the bosky head, down there the long straddling legs; and here in the midst of her the breast where we hear the beating of the mighty heart. Well then, nor I nor my fellows, to be sure, but the spirit that moves us, will make of this city the very image of a new creation, drawn forth from the spirit of mankind and from the bowels of created things, a manifestation of the munificence of heaven, and a witness to it. Hence will shoot forth such a spark as will set the world aflame . . ."

When he spoke in this manner his eyes would shine; nor did I dare to contradict him. Indeed, to oblige him, I reached the point of being his apprentice in this and in other even more fanciful predictions, myself party to no doctrine but witness to all. As when at Ménilmontant I mingled with the crowd of Saint-Simonians, dressed up in the same uniform as them – an open-breasted blue smock, a waistcoat laced down the back, and flame-red trousers. Extravagances which, amid the dedicated fervour of all present, forced from me a tell-tale laugh, induced me to headlong flight. It was that unforeseen laughter, the first for many years, which in my heart instilled a hope: that in the company of Secundus, and naïvely imitating his way of life, I might use it in some way to fill the interstices of my own. As one who with a drop of vinegar gives relish to the most insipid of dishes . . .

So I started to involve myself in his doings, even in the most insignificant things. In this manner I became a devotee of the chessboard, on which he excelled, and would accompany him to the café flattered at the chance of sitting beside him and with firm partisanship delighting or despairing at the fluctuating fortunes of each game. So reduced was I to begging for small emotions and contenting myself with them, much as a sailor hopes for even the lightest of breezes, to escape from the snares of a dead calm . . .

It was to one of these very occasions that I owe the event which revolutionized my life and assigned to me the destiny of which the final outcome is tonight impending.

I had gone with Secundus, as was my wont, to the *Café Régence*, where the great La Bourdonnais was taking on all comers. Among those who stepped forward to challenge him, along with the other leading players in the place, were my brother and a retired colonel of dragoons, a certain Pibrac. This man was a fierce royalist – nay, a legitimist – in whose skull a silver plate covered the crack from an old sabre-wound: a souvenir of Waterloo, where he, a Frenchman, had fought against the French.

The latter, in not succumbing, was alone among the opponents of La Bourdonnais, and he bragged about it later at the expense of Secundus, who himself had been an honourable loser. Whence arose diverse bantering remarks and the eruption of a contest between the two of them – in three games, on the understanding that the loser should, at the discretion of the other, shout out "Long live this" or "To hell with that," in violation of his most cherished beliefs.

It was indeed the custom, among the votaries of the game, to make use of these encounters to vent the frenzy of their ideals. As if the battle between those little boxwood men were the shadow of another and far more bloody one; one embodying the protagonists. It was therefore no rare thing for a player, according to his political persuasion, to insult the enemy pieces he captured with the name of Thiers, or of Cavagnac, or that of the sovereign himself . . .

Came the evening fixed for the encounter, and the game began, in a silence pregnant with suppressed exclamations, amid spectators very far from neutral standing solemnly at the backs of the two players. Among the many, La Bourdonnais himself, together with the rival champions Des Chapelles and Saint-Amant, the latter fresh from his triumphs in London. Spectators, these, who differed from the others in that they cared less for the passions implicit in the contest than for the expertise of the moves.

More or less equal in skill, were Pibrac and Secundus, but of contrasting temperaments. The former was pig-headed and cautious, obedient to the theories of the English school of play, whereas Secundus was imaginative and dashing in his strategies, capable alike of the most reckless inventions and the shrewdest sacrifices. One of which, ill-calculated, led to his submission in the opening game, while in the following game another sacrifice enabled him to level the reckoning.

The final trial was thus upon them. My brother, the worse off both in pieces and in position, seemed doomed to inevitable defeat. Nevertheless, his two fists under his chin and his temples throbbing painfully, he persisted in hatching I know not what decisive series of moves. Silent, tense, ferocious, was the attention surrounding them. Too inexpert at the game to be able to predict the solutions, I sought a denial of my fears in the faces of the bystanders. Pibrac disheartened me, though, by composing his lips into a derisive sneer, lighting a cigar the while, and allowing billows of smoke to sting the clear eyes of Secundus. I felt like remonstrating with him, but my brother stepped in before me. I saw his pallid, blue-veined hand seize one of his own pawns, then dirty its head in the overflowing ash-tray which Pibrac had before him.

Then, "With this marked pawn," he said; "with this grubby, plebeian pawn, I shall checkmate your king on the seventh move."

And he counted out the first of them.

I glanced at Pibrac. Sweat had sprung suddenly from his hair and brow, spread to his lips and side-whiskers. Mechanically he mopped at them with his hand: a short, stubby hand thick with reddish bristles, which finally we watched come to rest on his silver skull-cap like a hairy tarantula. The other hand, his left, begrudgingly shifted the pieces as Secundus imposed on him one check after another.

For six whole acts the tragedy dragged on, until Pibrac's king immured himself behind his subjects and there was smothered to death after a last and seventh move, which was made by the pawn crowned with cigar ash. In the silence that followed my brother's soft voice was heard to say *Voilà*, while the onlookers burst into interminable applause.

Pibrac seemed bewildered for a moment, then, throwing back his head, he rose.

"Monsieur," he said. "You touched this pawn some moves ago in order to besmirch its head. You then replaced it on its square. But your next move was not this pawn, as it should have been according to the rules. You moved a different piece, monsieur, and therefore you have lost."

We were appalled, myself and all the rest of them. But La Bourdonnais elbowed his way forward, with his massive frame and that square-jawed honest face of his. He took up Pibrac's king (the White) in his two handsome strangler's hands, raised it, and addressed it with mock solemnity.

"Your Majesty," he said. "I ask your pardon, but I see you as dead and buried."

Then, turning to the colonel, he continued in didactic tones: "Your complaint against the infraction ought to have been made at the time, Colonel. Since you waited until the conclusion of the game you are obliged to accept defeat. And now . . ." (he here pulled out his pocket-watch) "there being excellent reasons for thinking that it is about to strike midnight, we should wend our ways homeward without more ado. *Ego locutus, causa finita.*"

All present held their breath, as the two men stood face to face, both in the grip of emotion: the one of wrath, the other of exultation. But the spectators did not stir, as they waited for the public exaction of the pledge. Secundus turned to the dragoon.

"I exonerate you, monsieur," he said. "But let me tell you that the forfeit you would have had to pay was merely to shout out 'Down with tyrants!' Something more lenient than the 'Long live the king!' which you undoubtedly intended to inflict upon me, had I lost. 'Down with tyrants!', you will agree, rings somewhat milder and does not force one's conscience to violate its oath. Unless, of course, you consider King Pear to be a tyrant . . ."

I laughed, even I, for though I had not been in France for long I had often enough seen caricatures, both in the newspapers and posted on the walls, making fun of the king by depicting him in the form of that fruit.

No laugh from Pibrac. Instead, livid with rage, he drew an écu from his pocket, gave a swift kiss to the image of the king thereon, then moved towards the door.

All seemed to be over, but then, already on the threshold – goodness knows what waspishness suddenly got into him – he wheeled abruptly and retraced his steps.

"Now it is your family's turn to heap ashes on their heads!" he bawled, and with his glove struck Secundus on the cheek.

In the commotion that followed I hastened to thrust myself between the two, but the worst had already happened: satisfaction inevitably had to be demanded and granted.

"I do not seek out quarrels," declared Secundus with dignity, "but now and again they discover me. My seconds will call on you in the morning."

I was surprised to hear him speak in such a way. I could have sworn that he would on principle have refused to fight a duel; and, what is more, against such a man as that. It therefore occurred to me that, precisely as I was striving to imbibe his soul and to infect my own with it, so he for his part was doing likewise, and unwittingly imitating the most inane obligations of my status as a nobleman.

I attempted every means of dissuading him from the duel. I protested that he was inexperienced with weapons, whereas his opponent was a swordsman. The only point he conceded was that he preferred pistols to cold steel – inevitably he would be run through – while he pinned his hopes on his antagonist's failing eyesight.

"Come now," said he reassuringly. "True, I didn't invent gunpowder, but I do have two good eyes and know how to use them when need be."

Thereupon he retired to write his Will.

On the eve of the encounter the weather held memorably fine and bright, even though the winter was almost upon us. I recall the walk we took, my brother and I, through the principal streets of the capital, and the playbills at which I stole a glance, with the thought that he too was eyeing them and thinking to himself, "Who knows if I shall ever again see Madame Saqui dance on the tightrope, or ever listen again to Fréderique Lemaître in *Robert Macaire* at the *Théâtre des Folies* . . . Who knows where I shall be at this time tomorrow . . ."

All this was churning within me, I must confess, with a perturbation that was not solely anguish but also an eagerness for some imminent revelation; as if that duel were the terrible but necessary catastrophe that would unravel all the tangles, not only in his life but in my own.

Dawn broke, with a sudden chill, as the season dictated. We made our way to the Bois de Vincennes in a fly. In my pocket I was fingering the wafer-sealed package containing his last wishes.

As I jumped down, I remember, my boots were degged with dew and a fine mist pricked at my nostrils. For a moment I had hopes that it would thicken up, making the duel impossible. But in a trice it was dispersing, and to the seconds I dared not even mention the matter. Two to each side, these were, and singularly ill-matched: grim, ramrod-backed veterans were those of Pibrac, whereas ours were young, sleep-laden, half fearful, and half merry as on an outing. The formal attempt at reconciliation was superfluous.

"No reconciliation on the field," snapped Pibrac, adding: "I would have pardoned an insult to myself, but to my king, never!"

And one of his seconds: "I am confident you have not made me rise with the lark for nothing."

Pibrac removed his hat and bent to lay it on the grass. A ray of the newborn sun, piercing the dense screen of cloud, glinted on the silver plate that topped his skull. Viewed thus against the light the colonel seemed decked out with a saintly halo. But I had no time to curse myself for this unpardonable blunder before he desanctified himself of his own accord.

"If I die," he said, addressing Secundus, who stood face to face with him, "my last thought of you I wish to be this!" And once, twice, he flung him an obscenity.

In the meantime the weapons had been loaded, the distance agreed upon. Thirty paces between the two, who were permitted to take five more before shooting. But each was enjoined to halt after his opponent's shot and instantly return fire.

"I have the impression," whispered my brother, "of being in charge of my own execution."

At that point, somewhat tardily, the doctor arrived. He was a small, flabby man with a bored, impatient air. He hastened to declare the amount of his honorarium, then sat down on the pistol-case for a smoke.

Nothing further was lacking. The seconds counted out the paces, all in a body, though not without one brief dispute, since the younger of our two, having very long legs, attempted to extort another yard or two of distance. Finally, the order was given to take up position; although it was necessary to repeat this, on account of Secundus, who had loosed off a shot at random by putting too much pressure on the trigger.

These unforeseen occurrences, spiced with comedy, appeared to rid the scene of any possible fatal outcome, for it was unimaginable that acts and ceremonies as artificial as these could conclude other than with the drop of a curtain and a round of applause. I was even more sure on feeling a heavy raindrop fall on my nose, sign of a prohibition from on high. I looked up and saw a swollen flotilla of clouds which, having blotted out the sun, raced towards us like a jumble of monstrous rumps and snouts. A devastation of thunder and lightning then plummeted upon the darkened treetops.

"Quick!" I yelled out. "Run for cover!" hoping that the two duellists would follow me; but they remained motionless at the two edges of the clearing, their cheeks streaming, and in their eyes a stubborn madness. So utterly motionless (while the rest of us, like holiday schoolboys, were already huddled beneath the umbrella of the trees) as not to disturb a hare, which almost touched first the one and then the other as it loped the length of the clearing before sheltering in the cleft of a tree.

We yelled out again as we saw them, assailed by the cloudburst as by a volley of stones, advancing with slow steps to the firing line. I realized at that instant that Secundus wanted to die, and that I myself secretly wished him the same, however much I was clamouring to avert it.

Of what happened next I preserve little memory, but two images of my brother remain with me, ineradicable: with his arm raised in the act of shooting at a cloud, on his face an expression of childlike joy; and then, flat on his back in a welter of blood so tremendous that there was no telling where to look for his nose, or his mouth. It was like a carnival mask, or a grape-harvester's jestingly juice-smeared face. Nothing, in a word, that would have made one think of a death.

He had, in fact, died on the instant. For many years in my waistcoat pocket I preserved the scrap of lead which had shattered his jaw. But from that day on, whenever I hear a clap of thunder, I feel a steel hand crush my heart, and I hurl myself to the ground and tremble. Despite the fact that it is that very day, and that death in a downpour, which I have to thank for my recovery, for my rebirth. Yes: for the miracle was that by that murderous bullet I was rebaptized. At the instant that detonation annihilated Secundus, a second detonation, though it shed no blood, burst and reverberated in my own body, while my every fibre sang out in sudden relief. I, Conrad Ingafù, Baron Letojanni, the torn-in-twain, the torn-to-a-shred offspring of a noble race, behold me now emerge anew from that cocoon, that corpse there laid at my feet, and over which, both hypocritically and sincerely, I wept. Having until that time lived as a parasite at his expense, almost as if I had hired him to live life for the two of us, now that he was no more I garnered his soul into my own, and appointed myself the surrogate of his unaccomplished destiny. Thenceforward, being readmitted to the brotherhood of those who live, I would make mine the years that should have fallen to his lot; to act and to speak as he would have done; and to die, at the end, the death he was destined to die. If, before, he had vicariously usurped my being, from this moment on it would be my turn vicariously to usurp his . . .

Secundus himself had foreseen precisely this in his funerary epistle, of which I know every word by heart, and which ran thus:

Conrad, if you are reading these present lines, it will mean that I have eluded the grip of individual being, and am roaming at large and eternal in ethereal space. Expect no worldly goods from this testament of mine, it being denied to younger brothers, as well you know, to possess such things. Mark that I might have called you to task over these misapportioned birthrights. But to what end, if in the first instance I call them empty and vain? Never could I have consented to live at Court, to bleed our peasants white while flaunting a title as absurd as it is shameful. But this I will say to you: rid yourself of all you have, for to continue my work is all the legacy you need.

I can scarcely tell you how well this message chimed in with my desires. My brother's death, as I have told you, was for me a resurrection, and a second baptism. Each and every particle of my body was already working to that end. Bearing to him a natural resemblance in feature and shade of hair, I now found that even my larynx was attempting his cadences, so that the least trick of speech of his became day by day more natural to me. No need to beg leave of admittance, for I found myself at once, with his very own cloak about my shoulders, slipping in to the meetings of the Aphasmeni, of the Sublime Perfect Masters, persuading them here and discouraging them there, having become – hey presto! – eloquent in many tongues.

Nor did the few who knew, nor the many who were ignorant of it, ever regret this exchange of identities, so entirely did I take over that half which was absent. And this so naturally as to lose my own personality in it . . . save upon days of thunder and lightning.

In this manner I became the master-weaver of plots among the exiles of all the nations of Europe. Subsequent to which, for the last few years I have been with you in Cispanania, in the Capitanata . . . And always under the orders of *God the Father*, just as Secundus would have been, had he been able. And I have taken, as you know, the nick-name of Didymus, which in the Greek tongue means double, or twin, in honour of his distant shade. For he it is who ever commands me, I know not with what voice or breath breathed into me, or by what hidden ways he passes from his darkness to our daylight . . .

Nor, having in a short time to die, do I have any sadness but this: that when my head falls his will fall also. Nor any consolation either, except that when I die, those things that were reft and riven apart will become once more united.

EIGHT

Of Walking on Rooftops

The storm had blown itself out. As if hacked into a hundred pieces by the swish of a gigantic sabre, the cowling of black clouds permitted stars to reappear here and there between the shreds. Mingling with the succulent damp of the soil, the air grew sultry. One last rumble of thunder, deprived of vehemence, like the growl of a well-fed mastiff, was heard fading away far out over the water, where sea and sky raised a single barbican of darkness.

Thick night, persistent, ubiquitous. What hour it was they could not tell. They had missed the second changing of the guard, which had certainly taken place in the interim, though wholly drowned by the crashing of the storm. The baron was anxious.

"I didn't exceed my time, did I?" he asked.

But Agesilaos, from a scrutiny of the sky, concluded that it was scarcely past one in the morning. Which was indeed the period appointed for the gaolers below to rest and dry their clothes around a fire, before setting to to hammer the last few nails into the scaffold.

A fact soon confirmed by renewed sounds rising from the yard; not, however, further hammering, but a half-muffled voice telling a joke to a ring of listeners, followed by a loud burst of laughter wrathfully cut in upon by a slamming of shutters from the officers' quarters.

"Thinking over your story, *signor barone*," said the soldier,

"I take leave to wonder whether the code of honour provides for the postponement of a duel in driving rain."

"Such arguments are of little import," was Saglimbeni's view, "in a duel such as this, in which one of the antagonists wishes at all costs to kill, and the other at all costs to die."

Thereupon they all began to discuss the case of Secundus and the baron, and their mysterious identity of substance.

"Speaking for myself," put in the friar, "if I may be allowed to comment on the matter from a religious point of view, it would seem to me that the twins, so inextricably entwined, compose a Sacred Double, a Sacramental Duality, to which, if we adjoin *God the Father*, we immediately have a Trinity of Freethinkers, of the type that sends adolescents into ecstasies, with the Death and Passion of the Son, in order to redeem the human race, in the rain in the Bois de Vincennes."

This angered the baron. "Such witticisms do not appeal to me," said he. "Nor can I follow your sudden shifts from piety to sacrilege."

"If I masquerade as a friar," said Brother Cirillo, "it is not to make mock of the cloth, but rather out of frustrated love of it. I am a God-fearing man, even if I often inwardly call that same God to account for this world and the injustices of it. But none the less, tonight, while I am girding up my loins to speak to Him at closer quarters, I cannot restrain in myself a spurt of acidity, a rasping note, a friction, as when we scratch a fingernail across a pane of glass, or when the silk of an umbrella brushes our hair and our nerves cry out . . ."

"I understand," said the baron. "And I can also understand why my story might have seemed unbelievable to you, or downright laughable. Whereas the truth is to the contrary."

"Laughable it may well be," agreed Brother Cirillo, "but not unbelievable. It is merely that I have not yet fathomed whether you in this adventure were Jacob or Esau . . ."

Then, of a sudden, Narcissus fell on his knees. "Every one

of you," he cried, "has forgotten the only thing that matters, the ballot-box on the table where in a little time we have to place our life or our death. The cunning of the very devil it was to hand us this candle that burns down and down until it burns our fingers. In addition to this, our discourses, to which I had looked for help, are having the opposite effect. You, baron, who seemed so solid and self-confident! I now find you to be another man's proxy and, so to speak, his ghost in our midst. But be you the whole or the half of a man, you reinforce my doubt as to whether I am living a fairy-tale or dying a death that will make history. For pity's sake," – and he here burst into tears – "tell me what I must do! Justify this sacrifice or give me back to my youth, to the brimming glasses beneath the pergola, the music, the kisses. Let me live . . ."

"This terror of yours," said the baron, "is as of someone walking along a high cornice who trembles at the thought of falling. The thought terrifies, if combined with the sensation of great height, whereas no one is frightened of walking along a narrow wall three foot high, albeit the likelihood of falling is equal in either case. Thus you will observe that sailors, steeplejacks and sleepwalkers, inured by practice or secure in ignorance, survive without turning a hair; whereas the thinking man falls."

"But I . . . but all of us . . ." said the young man, "we are not only staring into the abyss, we are certain, very soon, to plummet into it. With this thorn in our flesh: that if we wished to we could step back."

Saglimbeni placed his hands on the lad's shoulders.

"Hush!" he said. "We'll pull the threads together in the end. As for your confession, baron, Narcissus is right: it doesn't help us to make up our minds. Not only that, but it avoids the most serious issue, one we have all been skirting around since we have been in prison, never daring to come out with it, but screening it behind extenuating phrases. I am talking about the innocent people killed in the explosion of our infernal machine, while the tyrant went unscathed. And I am talking about the further deaths which will be caused by the next such machine . . ."

"Have I not already said," murmured the baron, "that it needs the blood of martyrs?"

"Martyrs of their own free will, so be it; but not those who neither choose nor understand."

"And me, what about me?" put in Narcissus. "I who wish to be neither martyr nor informer."

His answer came as noises from the yard: the tramp of feet, a short exchange of words, the click of fixing bayonets.

"Have done now, the break-period is over," said Agesilaos, pricking up his ears. "And my tale may well be the longest."

At which, without waiting for consent, he announced, "My story I shall call 'The Hotchpotch'."

NINE

The Soldier's Tale, or,
The Hotchpotch

I was born thirty years ago on a table in a posting inn, or at least so I was told when I had reached the age of discretion. My mother was a strolling player touring from place to place in company with two brothers and a younger sister, Ramira. They used to act for a pittance before the most simple-minded yokels, performing in village squares, in warehouses, on threshing floors. They journeyed on foot, heaving at the shafts of a great wagon of wonders, laden with supplies both domestic and fantastic – tin swords and besoms all higgledy-piggledy, sacks of dried beans resting on the ramparts of a cardboard castle . . . This was their mode of travel, and if, as some philosopher says, travel broadens the mind, then my mother and uncles broadened theirs a good deal. They were always together, except occasionally at midday when the purse was empty, and the menfolk went off into the fields in search of some gypsy resource of green stuff and berries. Until one midday out of many, while the two women waited where the wagon, reaching skywards with its two gaunt arms, offered shade and shelter, a hussar came galloping up and, having secured his horse to a pinetree, in a trice stopped their mouths with kisses. Sweaty and hairy he was, and dusty at that scorching time of day. My mother was not so spotless as to take fright, though in a whisper she did beg the man to spare the young girl. Receiving nothing in reply but blows with the fist and jabs with a dagger, "Run for it!"

she cried to her sister, and with her teeth she tore off the man's earlobe. The girl made good her escape, she herself submitted to the force of the intruder, and I was born seven months later, prematurely and doubly unlooked-for, since all around had been blind to the gradual swelling concealed by my mother's voluminous stage costumes.

It happened on a Sunday evening, in the midst of a performance, when my mother, in the role of I know not which Stuart, must needs mourn over the body of a slain lover. Scarcely had she opened her mouth in the make-believe wailings of her part than she was seized with the genuine pangs, so that they were obliged to carry her into the nearby outhouse where the grooms and drovers lodged, and there, on a trestle table, help her to deliver.

Such were the time and place of my first appearance in the world, and ever since, years ago, I received a report of them from an eyewitness, I have often turned to musing on them between sleep and waking. Since that time, whenever I close my eyes, I gauge the height of the roof-beams, black with soot, above my newborn head; I sniff the stench of straw and wine, and visualize the woman, legs apart upon the mattress; I see beside her the bowl of blood, and hear the well-wishing applause of the bystanders. To one side, in a wedge of shadow, with backs to the wall, stand my two uncles, incredulous, white-faced, silently hating the handful of flesh which was me. However, they had no occasion to set eyes on it again. The following day they insisted on getting on the road, and that my mother should pause for a moment at the revolving hatch of the monastery of the Caracciolini Fathers to consign the infant therein. A few weeks later the two brothers finished up with stones round their necks in the river, following a brawl in a smuggler's den.

These are things which I have ascertained indirectly, and

are as a dream to me. In general I am extremely doubtful about the reality of events, and even about my own existence; nor do I cease to believe myself a dream. How much more so, then, that frippery of figures and acts, of gestures and odours, which regard my birth, the revelation of which came to me vouched for by the memory of another, while it is denied to mine . . . That remembrance, look you, both mine and not mine, seems to me as fleeting as a criss-crossing of shadows on a wall, two passers-by brushing shoulders and the sun catching them both aslant. Sometimes I wonder, does what I have forgotten exist? And my own death tomorrow, will that still exist when the eyes that witnessed it are no more? I mean the eyes of the guard, of the Governor, of the headsman . . .

"Don't leave out the headsman's daughter," put in the poet saucily.

As I was saying, (continued the other, passing his palm across his brow, for he had suddenly begun to sweat profusely), I therefore grew up in a seminary, and not a day of it but I imagined my destiny to be that of a priest. I was not unhappy about this; and indeed, the notion I had of the world was composed solely of orphans and priests. Orphans were my contemporaries with whom I studied and played, and orphans to my eyes appeared (though perhaps they truly were so) the adult priests who took care of us. Orphaned, male, black-clad: such for many years was the world around me.

The monastery lay in a deep valley ringed about by green uplands; and inhabited by austere black-clad men. The village was not far off, but none of us was allowed to go there. The shape that women are I learnt from a painted wax effigy of the Madonna, abandoned in the sacristy. I often went to gaze at it, to talk to it. I gradually came to believe that women were made of the same stuff as angels, something soft and feathery, which my hand would seek for in the air as if it sought to caress a cloud.

Soon I learnt, from the Life of Christ, that there were such things as fathers and mothers, and mothers who had never had "knowledge of man". It occurred to me to ask whether I too had had a mother, and whether she were of the latter kind. The silence I had for reply was frightening, and for some time I bore it around with me as if it were a hump on my back.

All this while I was growing, growing tough and hairy. One day, as I was singing in the choir, I heard my voice go gruff in my throat, and then disagreeable, like a grown man's. That morning my companions came flocking about me, hovering between disgust and fascination. They seemed like lambs that had heard the howl of a wolf. I need hardly tell you of the wretched practices which I gave myself up to shortly afterwards. Things that came naturally to me, and which I taught to my acquiescent companions. Not but that in the doing of them each one of us was gripped, and rendered speechless, by a deathly sense of annihilation. For a year or two this secret was a bond between us, an aureole surrounding us, although a melancholy one, tinged with guilt.

Everything we felt in those days was in fact two-fold. On the one hand, remorse and a yearning for death, on the other a surge of heroic, superhuman energy; on this side the horror of a solitude we all shared, on the other the exhilaration of waging war, just the few of us, each on his own against the rest of mankind. That, for us, was being fifteen years old.

But for me there was also a sense of being removed from everything that happened, as if each morning I were watching a dumb show of puppets, the relicts of an almost certainly invented life. I know that I am getting my words muddled up, but forgive me, for I can find no better. Certain it is that only at the moment of seeing the liquid spurt from the depths of me and spatter its albumen on the ground, only in that act did I feel such a grandiose exaltation that I was healed for a moment of the heartbreak of not being God . . . Our communal sinning was not long-lasting. I wearied of having as subjects those dull, reiterative simpletons, and shut myself up in the realm of my pleasure as in a disdainful conclave.

More time passed. I sought the panders I needed now in books. I remember a *Theologia moralis* in which my inexpert Latin examined the pages *de nuptiis dirimendis*, a *Theatrum mundi* in which every paragraph told of the nuptials of nymphs and gods; I remember the Testaments, both Old and New, with their Magdalens and Samaritans, and that Song of Solomon, of which I still remember the verses: "Thy hair is like a flock of goats, that appear from Mount Gilead . . . Thy lips are like a thread of scarlet, and thy speech is comely: thy temples are like a piece of pomegranate within thy locks . . . Thy two breasts are like two young roes that are twins, which feed among the lilies . . ."

I grew thin and hollow-eyed, and in my gaze was an obsessed and famished light. It was during this period that Don Carafa, a man of falsely jolly manner, who made a habit of sneaking up behind us and pinching us nastily, came looking for me on behalf of the Father Superior, Arrabito, who, laid low by a stroke, had long been confined to a chair in his room.

"He wants to see you," said Don Carafa. "I do not know why, but with gestures and occasional words he has several times requested a meeting." He lowered his gaze with unexpected unctuousness, and went on, "Be modest and obedient, whatever he may ask of you. Father Arrabito has always been a saint, but his illness has rendered him more saintly still."

I followed him in silence, though already bitterly rebellious. I had no love for either of these men, especially – and unjustly

– the elder of the two, since, with his mouth all contorted, he had had himself carried to Communion every morning on a litter, supported on either side by two of the burliest of us boys, of whom very often I was one; and I was obliged to watch his two lethargic gums slobbering over the sublime Presence of the Host as over a sugar jujube.

I obeyed for all that; and once before the seated man, and Don Carafa having been dismissed with a motion of the hand, I waited in fear and trembling for him to begin. The Father Superior was still *compos mentis*, although he usually stumbled over his words on account of the palsy that afflicted half his face. On this occasion, strangely enough, he spoke with sufficient clarity.

"Agesilaos," he began, "you have few friends among the fathers, and fewer still will you have when I am no more. And now that, having come precociously to manhood, you are already a nuisance in the choir, and to the innocence of the other boys, many are remembering the singular manner in which you came to us. Nor are we without those who, in this voice which nature has newly made to gurgle in your throat, perceive not the grown-up timbre of the years which are upon you, but some rasping ventriloquism on the part of the devil. Such is the price of being a gypsy-woman's child and born of an evil union. For which reason the time has come to acquaint you with these things, before others either distort or conceal them entirely."

He proceeded to tell me of my birth, and of the rumours concerning it which had passed between the neighbouring village and the monastery; then he fell silent.

When he recommenced: "Open that drawer," he commanded, pointing out a small cabinet. "You will find therein a piece of cloth containing the trifles that came with you fifteen years ago: a locket, a necklace of imitation emeralds, and a Toledo dagger, with lapis lazuli handle, skewered through a sheet of paper. It is on this latter that we found an indication as to your name . . ."

This speech, as I said, came smoothly from his lips, but I had no time to be surprised at this before his voice suddenly choked to a stuttering whisper, then died away altogether.

When I regained the corridor Father Carafa was in ambush for me, and started tugging at my sleeve.

"What's afoot? What did he want?"

I jerked myself free and ran off to my cell. There, having removed the wrapping from the motley legacy which it contained, I found considerable food for reflection. Starting with the necklace. This was a piece of completely valueless costume jewellery, ostentatious in its simulated regality; whereas the dagger, though embellished with precious stones, seemed of a murderous nature, assuming the dark spots staining the point to be blood rather than rust. Necklace and dagger, however, gave no further indication of themselves, except that the one had encircled the neck, the other armed the hand, of the mysterious Mary and Joseph who had, and I knew not how, brought me to the light.

From the other objects I learnt more. The locket revealed a blue-eyed visage, unutterably sad, traversed beneath the glass by two wisps of blondish hair. As for the message, I had scarcely unskewered it but I descried an almost undecipherable dedication: *To my son Agesilaos*; and below that two versicles, the first of which read, *Seek out the owner and you will find your father*; and the second, even more imperious, *Find this dagger a scabbard – in his heart!*

On reading these words I was seized by turmoil in my every limb. I was unable to fathom the motives which had led the Father Superior to this sudden act of revelation. Until that time, as was the case with the rest of the novices, I had heard only the meagrest whisperings concerning my birth: that it was unmentionable, illegitimate; that, no more nor less than my fellows, I was a foundling, crippled in both legs, lacking those two supports of father and mother which are the right of every son of man; but that in such a savage situation a remedy there was, and it was them, the worthy fathers: a hundred fathers instead of just the one. The Church, for its part, gathering me like a woman to her warm breast, would feed my forsaken orphanhood until it was sated. Thus had I grown up, with darkness and light intermingled in my mind: the son of none, but elevated to be a son of God, and destined to serve him.

But you will understand that in some way I now felt amputated from my new family, without having had restored to me my first, only a sample of which was proffered me, and that a troubling one . . . that blue-eyed portrait, that wisp of hair shut off by glass from the touch of my fingers, that needle-sharp dagger, that command to kill . . . I returned my inheritance to its wrapping and hid it under my pillow.

When I left my cell I found Father Carafa still on the qui vive, very nosy and wheedling.

"This really has to be squeezed," he announced, palping with mellifluous fingertips at a pimple on my chin. Then, with insistence, "What did the Superior say? What did he want with you?"

"I am bound to secrecy," I answered shortly. "Holy Obedience demands it." And I slipped from his grasp.

A few days later Father Arrabito died, and the protective hand which, however frail and tacit, he had held over my head, now withered and left me defenceless. Whether it was that one of my companions had accused me, or that my confessor or someone else's had betrayed the secrecy of the confessional, or that on some article of underwear or at the bottom of the urinal they had discovered the tell-tale signs . . . the fact is that, albeit in ambiguous and nebulous terms of speech, I was taxed with acts of impurity and of instigating my companions to scandal. There followed an injunction to wash down my body twice a day with ice-cold shower-baths, to leave the door of the latrines ajar and my cell windows open wide. In my cell, sometimes by day but more especially by night, Don Carafa would rush in to take me by surprise, and with quick fingers pluck the coverlet from over me. Until one evening, as I stubbornly feigned sleep, I heard a soft puff of breath blow out the candle, and a step pause at the foot of my pallet, and felt a soft pudgy fleshiness insinuate itself beside me.

"Help! Murder!" I cried, kicking out, as a white nightshirt took to flight. When my companions came running, it was not hard to convince them that I had cried out in a dream.

But by this time I felt myself in disgrace within those monastery walls. Sometimes from the window I would watch the passage of birds, or the flight of clouds towards the rim of the horizon, and would feel my bare toes itching in my sandals. My beard had started to grow, and I had unwillingly complied with the order to shave it off. All the more so because the razor aggravated the pimples laying siege to my face. I would squeeze from them a humour, a pallid mucilage, that reminded me of the other, the seed spilt upon the ground. As if in the sepulchre of my body there lurked the superfluities of an infection, and I must help to drain them away.

Finally one day – and here I am approaching the most weighty incident of my life, from which derive all others, and even this death of mine derives – while I was making some order among the papers of the late Father Arrabito (a task set me as a penance), from one of the volumes dropped a sheet of paper. There, in the erstwhile handwriting of the owner, I found a summary of the 79 Errors of Baius, a name which was new to me, but which I soon discovered to be that of a theologian of Louvain and a leading influence on Jansenist doctrine. Written in faded, ancient ink, in malformed characters presumably due to the scribe being of tender years (and who else but Arrabito himself as a youth?), I was dumbfounded when I began to comprehend it. For in each proposition, and veiled no longer behind signs and symbols, I found my most secret thoughts, and in my heart there was born a proud dismay, like that of one who looks in the mirror and discovers on his breast a blemish, and knows not whether it be a birthmark, leprosy, or the mark of a regal fleur-de-lys.

So, in short, this heretic preached about an Adam resembling a great body made of light, existing in peace and felicity, and instinct with the love and understanding of God. Until the very moment of the severance, the Fall, when the human race, driven on by irresistible lust, did nothing but sin, knew nothing but sin; nor did it have any choice other than sin. Mankind was justly punished, therefore, for a sin it was compelled, even unwillingly, to commit . . .

So then, was not I myself that Adam? I the predestined, irremediable sinner, debarred from every Eden, fated to lose my way even as a prisoner between these walls.

Now, I don't know which of you are believers and which non-believers. In the midst of so much activity in the secular life we have never had time to touch on higher things. Maybe the only one who might understand me is Brother Cirillo, who has some knowledge of religion and feeling for it, but I doubt he has more understanding in this case than you have yourselves. The truth is that I am a believer, of a faith as blind and unremitting as that of a corpse; but that as far as salvation is concerned I throw myself upon the mercy of God, and no longer put trust in my own works, which are ineluctably fated to be evil. I think of the evil that I perpetrate as spreading around me like the weightless ether, and exuding from my skin in invisible driplets, emerging in the grime beneath my fingernails, the mucus of my nostrils, and even the cerulean liquor of my eyes. Sin is everywhere, I say – *omnia immunda immundis* – but in me above all others it is triumphant! Of this did Baius convince me, and all the more did I believe him, seeing that his words gave substance to my own thoughts; though of these I would only gain knowledge, as to whether they were substance or shadow, by going forth among men and putting them to the test.

So I had to get away. I didn't stop to think about it for more than a brace of shakes. We all know that the plans for an escape from gaol require even more detailed preparations than a marriage ceremony. I, on the contrary, threw myself into the enterprise as one hurls oneself from a bridge. And so one midnight, a small bundle on my back, the dagger in my pouch and my other maternal talismans concealed betwixt scalp and cap, I clambered over the gate and set off for the valley, trusting to luck.

It was August, and the sky was clear. I made good speed, following the only road there was, along which every morning I saw the tradesmen come, and which was therefore bound to lead me straight to the village. As the ground was hard and dry I took off my sandals and went barefoot, almost at a run. Not from fear of being followed, but in the jubilant certainty of being alive and free. I know now that every step I took in that escape brought me closer to this present funereal epilogue; but I have no regrets. The years I have lived since then, although not numerous, are well worth the decades I would have spent singing psalms in a monastery.

I reached the first houses some two or three hours later, by my reckoning. There was not a soul stirring, and I at once went off into reverie. Sitting down on the first threshold I came across, before a humble door, and stretching out my legs on the cool of the flagstones, through my half-closed eyelids I began to see mirages. It was not the first time that after some fatigue or fit of dizziness, with the aid of the

104

moonlight, my eyes had tricked me with visions. I was therefore not afrighted, or even astonished, by the amazing sights that appeared before me. Indeed I was almost tempted to applaud each tableau in the pageant: angels with curved sabres walking poised on the rooftops; a procession of old men, each one approaching me with misty visage, the type of face which glee does not make light, but loathsome; and, from the sea, drenched with seawaters, a head of hair that radiated and ramified after the manner of forked lightning, or as the light of a lamp is cast on a wall through a trembling curtain.

I was aroused by a muttering from beyond the door I had leant my head against. Some person, and the voice was a woman's, was mouthing vile oaths and calling upon them, to judge by the words I picked up here and there through the intervening panels, to defend her bed, if not from death itself, at least from cockroaches and mosquitoes.

I got to my feet and knocked. The silence that fell beyond the door was evidently fraught with suspicion, fear and curiosity. A minute went by before I heard a "Who's there?", and five minutes before the face of a dishevelled she-devil poked out through an opening to examine me, to divine whether I really was, as I maintained, a thirsty youngster asking nothing but a drink of water.

This ocular scrutiny must have resolved itself to my advantage, for the door opened, I was grasped by a voracious arm, and dragged into the dark. The hatch in the door, which was at eye level, had been left open to the moonlight, and it took me little time to put it to good use. In this one-roomed dwelling I made out miserable sticks of furniture, a jug, a stool, a cord stretched from one wall to the other whereon dangled a few rags; and finally a horsehair pallet on the floor, on which, minuscule of face and limb but endowed with abundant breasts, there lay an old woman, naked.

I was assailed by a doubt, whether she might not be a

105

sequel to my erstwhile fantasies, but I could not imagine what I might have modelled her on, since in effigies alone and never in living flesh had I yet looked upon a woman. But she had set to scrutinizing me, summing me up. From the way I was clad and the pallor of my face, from the odour of wax and of incense, she knew me at once for a seminarist.

"You've escaped," she concluded with a laugh.

She then banged shut the hatch, and I saw no more. Only her hands did I feel, trembling over me, fumbling, stripping me naked. Without a twinge of remorse I heard the rattle of iron and fake gold as my little treasury fell from my cast-off clothes and scattered across the floor.

But she: "Breath of my life! Breath of my soul!" she cried. "Who led you to my side this night?"

And with a thrusting tongue she parted my lips, she drew me into her, sucking me into the scalding cavern through a nimbus of nauseating euphorias.

Afterwards, lying beside me, no sooner had she learnt my name than she thumped a fist against her forehead, and, "I saw you born!" she claimed. "I was scullery-maid there in Master Antonio's pothouse, and I held your mother down on the planks, I gripped her by the braids, I drew you forth from her belly!"

And she told me of the play brought to a halt, the birth, the sudden departure the very next morning, and of how I had been left there in a basket, with "Agesilaos" for the name I should go by.

She told me nothing more, but fell into a stony sleep, crumpled like a rag in the grip of her wrinkles. She was still asleep when I got up, determined to make good my escape. By groping in the dark I had retrieved my belongings, and was about to slip softly away when I felt the urge to take another look at her. I have to confess that, down on my knees and aided by the moonlight from the door I had left ajar, with greedy eyes I returned, like an anatomist to a wound, to spy out, amid the thickets of the pubes, that terrifying crater . . .

In this manner I entered the game of life. It was the year, you should know, that war was afoot in Herzegovina, and volunteers were being recruited right, left and centre. When I reached the city, the soles of my feet cracked from the heat and exertion, wan from lack of sleep and makeshift meals, it seemed too good to be true when, by adding a year or so to my age, I found myself under arms, my belly fed, my body clad. And here I have to pause for a little while to explain, even to myself, what my state of mind was in that predicament.

This is how it was. Brought up to believe in an eternal Might and an eternal Spirit, but finding myself from the start shut off from the outside world, I had always been aware that there was a void within me, a sort of bottomless pit, that I would have to fill in with bunglings, disobediences, and vendettas. Against whom, I knew not. Being sensuous by nature, and inclined to believe that every pleasure is a crime, but that no crime is blameworthy, I had willingly given myself over to the paroxysms of voluptuousness, seeking in them more a challenge than a down payment on punishment. However, I soon realized that both punishment and challenge burnt themselves out in me to no purpose. I then attempted to search out less abstract targets, but the name I prayed to and cursed with deliberation every evening, with my mouth pressed into the pillow, and the flies I left to die imprisoned beneath an upturned glass, did not meet my needs, and merely made me feel but half a sinner.

At this point, providentially, came the two aforesaid discoveries: that in the matter of my birth there was someone faceless and nameless who was responsible, who deserved to be punished; and that all sins were inevitable, and therefore forgiven in advance. A curious contradiction: the warranty of forgiveness that I bestowed on myself I was careful not to grant in equal measure to my father, whoever he might be. Indeed, in my thoughts I combined disgust at his long past violence with the most tolerant indulgence towards my own violence to come. For which, furthermore, I sought more noble justifications than mere respect for a mother's commandment. A mother I had never seen, who might not even be still living, and to whose womb I felt bound by no sort of cord, except for that tiny locket. Whereas I was more anxious to confer on my passage through this earth a thing it sorely lacked: the illusion of a tragic purpose such as, for example, a parricide . . .

It was in such a frame of mind that each morning I gazed upon the face in the portrait, murmured the two lines of incitement, and in my pocket fingered the haft of the dagger. I was going to kill my father. The idea filled me with exultation. Nor, at bottom, had I become a soldier for any other reason than to train myself to kill; and because, to hunt my quarry down, it seemed to me best to move in the military circles to which he belonged.

I had learnt from Father Arrabito that I had been abandoned in March, and from the old woman's prattlings that the rape had taken place at the time of the grape harvest in the neighbouring district, when a troop of hussars was roaming the country there. Now, although so many years had passed, by putting suitable questions to the veterans one by one, I reached the conclusion that my quarry, fifty years old by this time, must be among the most senior officers in the Second Regiment, the same which was said to have so distinguished itself in the cavalry charge at Salonika.

At this point, distracting me somewhat from my purpose, I was seized by that craving for Liberty already current among the soldiery. Until that moment, though hostile to any form of oppression, I had never given a thought to the common destinies of mankind, dwelling exclusively on my own; nor to tyrants other than those within reach of my rancour – my religious superior or my sergeant. I now discovered that the world was cursed by more odious tyrants; and that, though remote, they were not invisible gods but people of flesh and blood, capable of bleeding should a steel blade pierce their throats. I was carried away by the notion of venting myself upon them with deeds which my vainglory even now fore-shadowed as famous. I therefore joined the Carbonari, deter-mined that as soon as I could I would act single-handed and, after killing my father, kill the king himself.

Judge for yourselves, my friends, whether or not I should be ashamed of having joined the conspiracy out of a pighead-edness which, even as I mention it, seems to me no more than the regurgitation of a perverse unhappiness. Certain it is that I applied myself zealously to this new notion, working to make myself expert in munitions and explosive devices, in the hope that one day my skill in such matters might in some way redound to my advantage.

Years passed. That war was scarcely over before the start of the next, that of the so-called Quadrilateral. The few survivors of the Second Light Cavalry were scattered among other units, and I had no means of pursuing the search for my father. I made up for this by falling to against my new enemies, indulging the pleasure of bearing, to their detriment, the three current banners of Liberty, the People, and the Republic.

I met you, baron, at that time; and you will certainly remember that evening, in a den near the harbour, while the saint's-day torches flared out in the streets and we, encellared and swathed in voluminous cloaks, sat planning the future. *God the Father* came in person, masked, and uttered not a word except to you, and then only a whisper in your ear. So essential was it for him to preserve the incognito of his voice, which was, as I later realized, the most instantly recognizable of his attributes. Other such evenings followed, but I am chiefly mindful of the first of them, for it was on the very next day, while I was officer of the guard at the gate of the barracks, that I saw an unknown horseman with the insignia of a colonel dismount before me and, with a curt nod, hand me the reins of his horse.

He was thick with dust from head to foot, nor was it easy to discern a face beneath that mask of grime. In spite of which, at the instant when he turned his head before striding off, I perceived, not without a thrill of deadly triumph, that the lobe of his right ear was missing.

I was convinced, by the moment of dizziness that made my eyes swim, that I was already home – close to the lair of my prey. I felt my blood singing as a river may sing, perhaps, when it feels its waters approaching the estuary. There he was, my kinsman and unaware of it, the flesh which I was heir to. There was his cruel mouth, so much like mine; there on his body was the imprint of the teeth of a young animal turned at bay . . . Hatred arose in my gorge, so entire and perfect that it might have been love. But in a trice I was cold and rational again, like a soldier with oil and tow polishing his gun on the eve of battle.

I soon learnt that he had come to raise volunteers to lead over the mountains in order to reconstruct the army. I presented myself without delay, and once at the front had little trouble in getting myself appointed his orderly and regimental standard bearer. In this way I gradually unearthed confirmations, if any were needed, of the years-old verity for which I was seeking. Until one morning I surprised him, while dressing, seated on his bedside and trying to force a boot onto a foot swollen with gout, his breeches undone and revealing the dark, pendulous, flaccid root of all my woes.

I revelled in delight in showing him the dagger studded with lapis lazuli, and asking him if in all his life before he had ever set eyes on it . . . I was still sitting beside the corpse when they took me, blood-spattered as a butcher.

This happened ten years ago. I need not tell you of my escape, the outcome of which is well known. Nor of how I then went roving the seacoasts working on ships and in arsenals, and everywhere kindling fires of patriotic disorder, at Marseilles, for example, among the refugees, and in Corfu when they tortured Ricci to death. At the same time I had recourse to the most ridiculous follies, bearding death when it was utterly unnecessary to do so. Over a trifling impropriety of speech, or to gain the favours of a woman I despised.

What more? The baron here plucked me away from single-handed exploits. Returned once and for all to my native land, I have been with you, and so shall I be at this supreme moment. But without truly understanding whether in the hotchpotch of my life I have been master or mastered; and whether, disguised as a martyr, there does not dwell within me a dissolute, fanatic barbarian . . .

TEN

The Zealous Headsman

At this point Agesilaos, as if the ticking of a clock had precisely measured out the duration of his discourse, stopped dead, and at the very same instant from the prison yard came the usual bustle that marked the changing of the guard.

"Three o'clock," said the soldier gently, while at the spyhole a glowering warder came peering in, and was surprised at the semi-darkness of the interior.

"We prefer it like this, not seeing each other," said the baron, forestalling him. "We are praying," he lied, persuading the man to withdraw, and then turning to Agesilaos.

"So the officer you murdered was your father," he said. "Or so you took him to be. That merciless act did not stem from civic wrath, as many of us have until now believed, but served purely to resolve a personal obsession . . ."

"An action," observed the soldier, "often has two or three motives, no one of which excludes the others."

"True," returned the baron, "but your story does not answer to the requirement; or else it answers in too many ways. Were you happy at the moment of escaping from the seminary? Or while castrating and massacring yourself in the person of your father? Or when you happened upon the fateful craving for liberty? Or in none of these cases? And then, this mania you have for hating yourself, which I (if you will forgive me) find utterly grim and abhorrent . . . And this pig-headed love-hate battle with God . . . I cannot find your life commendable, soldier. Worse than that, I do not understand it."

"I personally," said the student, "think that you are not so black as you have painted yourself, Agesilaos. That you grew up, immured in your monastery, a savage but a noble one. I will wager that the moment you had tracked down your quarry you rejoiced less than you despaired over that undertaking you had all but forgotten, and would have wished to revoke on. For if in that case . . ."

At this point he lost his thread, blushed, uttered not another word, and turned to the poet as if entreating him. And the poet, in a burst of kindness, stroked the lad's hair again.

"What has become of your locks, O Phaedo?" he declaimed, and no one could tell whether he was in earnest or in jest. But then he continued in more natural tones:

"My explanation is different," he said. "You, Agesilaos, were born not of harmony but of violence. The seed which thrust life into you by that very act transmitted to you the contagion of its own brutish nature. Your father, that is to say, made you his own ape, and for this he perished. You committed no parricide. Your father it was who made use of your hands to kill himself."

Brother Cirillo would stand for none of this.

"No!" he cried.

The old man seemed to have taken on a new lease of life, sharp of eye, and with that hypocritical voice of his and that turban of rags around his head, which gave him the air of an operatic caliph. Plainly he had managed to make himself felt among them, usurping some portion of authority from the baron, to such a pitch was he revealing himself in a light completely at odds with his accepted image – that of the perfect scoundrel. One thing was certain: that in spite of his unpleasant manner, he never ceased to intrigue them, and even somehow to dominate them.

"No!" he exclaimed again. "Personally I absolve this man. His career seems to me perfect. Coming inadvertently into this world, conceived in his own despite by violent loins, twice over has he suffered the gross abuse of his birth: firstly because, as in the case of every man, God did not ask his consent; and secondly, because his father did not ask such consent from his mother. How is he to be blamed if, unable to revenge himself on God, he did so on his physical pro-creator? If he decided to remedy one outrage with another . . . And if finally, he has sought from your shadowy *God the Father*, and from you who are his Evangelists, some obscure surrogate for his missing family? To him and to you others, and not to the Cause of the peoples of the world, for which, in spite of all appearances he cares little, he will sacrifice his head tomorrow in filial holocaust."

"Could that be true? Could my heart be the shambles you say it is?" asked the soldier, aghast. "And even if all you say were true, I only know that I feel up against the wall. I don't like living and I don't fancy dying. Chopped in two, what's more . . ." he concluded with a sigh, as he moved yet again to the vantage point of the window, whence the now fully-erected scaffold could be seen in the fluctuating light of the moon, according as she burst through the cloak of clouds or lurked in ambush. And the scaffold was a toy of wood and iron, smooth and strong, for giant children to play with. Not a soul in sight, for the moment. Perhaps the headsman and his acolytes were putting their feet up.

"I still maintain that I would rather be hanged," declared Agesilaos, and the trend of the conversation went off at a tangent. All of them, and he himself first and foremost, seemed to have lost interest in the adventures of the foundling, and they began to wrangle over the various methods of execution. Exactly as a man, when discussing the several beauties of a woman, shouts down anyone who dares to contradict him.

It was the friar who took the centre of the stage once more.

"I imagine that this eccentricity in putting the guillotine to work again is the Governor's doing. He is an implacable monarchist, and he must enjoy being able to use the very same coin to revenge the old idols of his youth, your Louis', your Marie-Antoinettes . . . He's just the type to revel in such symbolic retaliations and punishments in kind. Or maybe he's tired of being nicknamed trigger-happy old Sparafucile."

He was speaking in a strangely stentorian voice, unless it was the low ceiling that made it boom the more. Stentorian, but with a falsetto squeak every now and again. Like a contralto who has overtaxed her voice or is suffering from congestion of the lungs. And this gave the scene an operatic air, himself as soloist with anguished brow in the midst of an aria – Turk in Italy or Impresario from Smyrna – and the others grouped before him playing the part of chorus.

"At dawn," resumed the friar, and it was as if he were floating off into a cabaletta, "none of us will be alive, and neither right nor wrong will be of further avail. This does not grieve me. Inquisitive about life, I am equally so about death. So that quite unlike you" – and he turned to the soldier – "I would say that I am happy to be alive, but do not mind dying. Personally, everything I receive through my senses is a stimulation to me, whether it be pleasure or pain. Even the torture yesterday evening, with its agonies that still rack my every limb, starting with my forehead where they clamped on the 'crown of thorns' – yes, even torture has been a special emotion. This network within my body, of slender, twisting threads, my nerves, I mean; this violin of nerves which each time plays a different tune; so long as it vibrates I willingly let it suffer . . ."

"There's no accounting for tastes," put in the baron crisply.

"Here are we, thinking of ourselves as heroes, and there are you, preening yourself about taking pleasure in the most out-of-the-way experiences. Although death is an experience of which even the most incapable of us is capable . . ."

He fell silent, hearing the key turning laboriously in the lock. Then came a light, darting through the spyhole, a restless beam of light that probed the entire cell. The door opened, soldiers entered bearing torches, while from the wall the face of the Madonna once more looked down in sorrow.

A bodyguard had arrived, and all imagined that the Governor had come to claim his due of death or denouncement. But instead it was the executioner.

"Never fear now," declared Mastro Smiriglio, advancing into the room already crammed with men and lighted all too brightly. "The hour is not yet come. I am here to take measurements. I'll have you know that the gullet is sometimes leathery, and sometimes exceeds the limits allowed for by the aperture of the lunette. A personal fitting is called for. Tailors and cobblers, in their professions, do as much for their clients."

"Did you really have to come as soon as this?" came a mild protest from Agesilaos.

"I would far rather have gone to bed. But orders is orders, as the saying goes, and them as gives the orders doesn't sweat blood."

He was both jolly and obsequious, as ever. A well-known figure in the fortress, a Sicilian by birth, who as a lad had joined the retinue of Murat, and after that the king's; and who spoke three languages, all of them badly, peppering them with funereal jests and ingenuous vulgarisms, with the sole purpose of putting his patients at their ease. He now made his entrance in his Sunday best, clad, to swathe his incipient pot-belly, in a black satin waistcoat. His shoes were black and he wore black cotton gloves.

At the sight of him the five of them rose to their feet, Brother Cirillo with greater difficulty on account of his wounds and his age. Smiriglio approached him first, drew a measuring tape from his pocket, and with a swift movement encircled his Adam's apple.

"This may be a trifle over-scrupulous," he said, "but I like to do a clean job. I am not a common or garden cut-throat, but *l'exécuteur des grandes oeuvres de justice*, as is stated in my papers. I studied in France with Monsieur Simon . . ."

The condemned men remained standing, anxious to be rid of him, irritated by his chatter and by the intrusive throng. But he with phlegmatic efficiency lingered over comparing neck with neck, then turned to brood pater-nally from the viewpoint of the window on the apparatus below.

"*Oh, le joli bilboquet!*" he exclaimed, and immediately added: "She suffers from disuse, the poor darling. *L'avugghia – si nun cusi s'arrugghia*, as my grandmother used to say."

"A needle that sews not, rusts," translated Saglimbeni to himself, and then point-blank, not without some malice, "Have you a daughter, Smiriglio?"

He was disappointed when he heard the answer: "You can see her down there below. Her name is Louisine." And he pointed to the towering machine.

Then said the student, "Will it hurt, Smiriglio? I keep on asking, but nobody knows the answer."

The man smoothed down his waistcoat with one hand, while the other he held to his heart in a parody of emotion.

"It will be like drinking a glass of water," he replied. "You will feel it no more than if they had guillotined a stuffed dummy of you. And if I lie," he added, "come back tomorrow night and snatch the sheets off my bed."

"Be off with you!" The baron good humouredly bundled him away by the shoulders; and at last he went, not without

117

leaving in one corner, as was the custom, a bottle of anisette which none of them laid a finger on.

The cell plunged back into darkness, although the rectangle of the window had grown imperceptibly lighter.

"Four o'clock," exclaimed Agesilaos, while from below rose the familiar soldierly din.

"We have little time to waste, my friends," agreed the baron. "And during that time I am not forgetting our undertaking, which I would urge you to bring to a conclusion. You see how the night is languishing, and with it our last drops of life."

"Poet," commanded Brother Cirillo, as if he were the chairman of the meeting, "now the baton passes from the baron's hands to yours. It is your turn to tell us about yourself."

"Very well," said Saglimbeni. "I have a hundred thousand memories. I only have to make a choice. I will tell you my favourite, which is called 'The Blinded Cock'."

So he began.

ELEVEN

The Poet's Tale, or,
The Blinded Cock

While I was listening with one ear to the adventures of
Agesilaos, I was mulling over in my mind what I would tell
when my turn came, and what it was expedient to pick out
from the shattered mirror of my life: whether the least of
splinters or the sharpest one. When I was not tempted, quite
simply, to bid farewell to the world with one last, supreme
piece of humbug. You see, I grew up unable to distinguish
between truth and falsehood, falsehood and truth, like a fish
in the water of two intercommunicating bowls. To the point
of no longer distinguishing the wall of glass from the ether,
the cabal from real life. Of who I am, therefore, in essence,
and what a contorted nature is mine, it is not mere guile that
induces me to keep silent, but the very fact that I am the last
to make head or tail of it. I admit, into the bargain, to loving
clowns who carry around a mask of make-up instead of a face,
and are so convinced by the patches they deck themselves out
in as to become absolute forgers and impostors of themselves.

Perhaps it is owing to the foregoing defect, if not to this
other – of never having recourse to simple means to simple
ends, but complicating both the former and the latter – that
I enjoy the name of poet. Poet? Fiddlesticks! I read many
poets when I was young, and am well versed in operatic arias,
and when need be I can put together a couple of frolicsome
lines, but as for calling myself a poet . . . Although I must
say that I love the sinuous embraces, one with another, of

words; and their antiphonal responses, their melodious echoes of the stirrings of the heart. Thus, in the last few weeks you have oftentimes heard me declaiming the opening lines of *The Prisoner of Chillon*,

> Eternal Spirit of the chainless Mind!
> Brightest in dungeons, Liberty! thou art . . .

and whistling the chorus from *Fidelio*, to which the condemned men climb from the abyss up into the light. If only to cherish the fond hope that we also might be granted an equally miraculous deliverance. Melancholy diversions these, I admit, since in equal measure with you I hear the murmuring of the hours as they flow towards the end, while nothing avails to defer their unflinching plunge . . .

Be that as it may, let me come to the point. I leave it to you to decide whether I am cooking up a dish of lies, and whether there be more credibility to be attached to my love of ennui than to the relish in crime and wickedness to which Agesilaos treated us a while ago . . .

You will, above all else, have to return with me in time, to imagine me as I was at twenty years old, eyes full of a beguiling light, alive with the promise of infallible happiness. Not that I put overmuch trust in the glances the ladies gave me, but truly I must have been handsome, proud and confident in my good looks. To which still greater value was added by the most legendary rumours concerning my daring, my passionate love of liberty, my Pimpernel-like vanishing acts between bedroom and barricade, bearing always a flower in one hand and a gun in the other.

As such, or imagined as such, I entered the Grand Duchy to stir up the nobility against the tyrant. The nobility, I repeat, not the common people. For the envy and ambition of the few can add more fuel to the flames of insurrection than can the indigence of the many. It had therefore already been necessary to confer with Torremuzza and with Romeo, sometimes in cities, in secret places, at others in remote country districts which I reached on horseback beneath the scorch of the sun, and where my guides were field-guards with sullen looks and sudden smiles.

Thus, after a day's journey, I found myself at the foot of the great volcano, whither I had been summoned by urgent letters from Duke Maniace, even now on his deathbed with a tumour of the throat. I had been long on the road, I recall, in a dazzling furnace of dust, pausing from time to time in the shade of some carob tree, as at the stages of a profane *via crucis*. The lava on either side of the sheep-track might have been disgorged that minute from jaws of iron by some fossilized dragon who beneath his eyelids conserved, unextinguished, the flash of the primal *fiat lux*.

Finally, in a stone hut at the foot of a hill we allowed ourselves a longer rest, while a farm labourer peeled us half a dozen prickly pears and let us drink our fill from an earthenware pitcher of ice-cold water. Then, even as I was wiping my mouth, I was surprised by a hushed conversation, the exchange of a few swift words, accompanied by almost imperceptible conniving gestures. I pretended to have noticed nothing, but promised myself to keep a sharp eye open. To no avail. We had scarcely set off again but, as I raised my eyes to make out the first inklings of the ducal residence upon the hilltop, my two escorts wheeled around, set spurs to their mounts, and without more ado were lost in a blaze of sunlight. All it then needed was for the perfidious beast that bore me to become restive in turn, anxious to toss me out of the saddle and canter off to join its friends. I could have controlled it nevertheless, had it not been for that stone, so unequivocally placed in the middle of the road as to suggest a centuries-old conspiracy betwixt the rim of that rock and my frontal bone.

I regained my senses in a spacious bed-chamber fragrant with fresh linen. The faces looming over me were those of a woman and of a young lad.

Of all the eyes I ever saw, hers were the blackest: two moist, tenebrous gems in which the most mineral inertia wedded the most liquid of languors. Eyes you might expect to see pass in an instant from feigned sleepiness to swift rapacity and plunder, darting beneath the visor of her long, long lashes with the flash of a reptile snatching at its prey.

I felt those eyes upon me even before I opened my own, such was the ferocity with which they pierced the barricade of unconsciousness. When at length I saw them clearly, I was seized alike by terror, astonishment, and delight. The very same feeling a dove has, spellbound by a serpent.

Black were the eyes, the face athirst and lovely, though lightly marked by smallpox; the expression was one of hunger tempered by some hidden restraint; the hands eager to flutter over any object in the vicinity, never content to stay in the shelter of the sleeves . . . Lastly the dress, which was black from head to foot, a sumptuous mourning costume from which I divined an unequivocal message: the duke was dead and my mission strangled at birth. This was his widow and that, so pallid of face, his scarcely pubescent heir. Too green to be capable, even if willing, to inherit his father's commitment to our conspiracy.

As for my guides, and the way they deserted me, I now knew what to think. Having learnt from those furtive whisperings of the death of the duke their master, they had felt relieved of the obligation to escort me any further, as if, from one moment to the next, I had become an excrescence to be voided, no longer a guest to be cosseted but an outrage to the modes of speech and conduct which my presence violated.

This I realized only vaguely, feeling myself all the more a stranger in this bed. I was all this while in pain. Under the bandages my head was throbbing, although the single blow which had rendered me unconscious had not been of too severe a nature. Worse by far was the thirst: a writhing of all the fibres which fever had set ablaze like flames in a stubble-field. None the less I steeled myself to prevent the escape of a cry for help, since prudence demanded that in my present situation I should make up my mind what position I should adopt before regaining my senses in public.

I therefore closed myself up in darkness once again, though not before I had taken in at a glance, in addition to the two faces, all the visible details which my optic nerve permitted me: a lofty ceiling of lath and plaster traversed by dark beams from which, by the neck, hung wooden puppets of Paladins and bags bursting with toys, as befits a young boy's room; and then, at the foot of the bed, the french windows on to the terrace, framing an indescribable sky in the indigo rectangle of which – candelabrum of creamy petals – an agave plant soared upwards.

I deceived nobody with my fictitious swoon, for the signs of my having come round were all too obvious. So that the room rang with a husky "Saglimbeni!", and in those few syllables there was a certain intimacy, something between the wifely and the maternal, which between myself and this woman, as in the Middle Ages when the children of two rival kings married each other, sealed a rainbow covenant of peace and a pact of blood.

Thus began the most boring and blissful five weeks of my life. As a convalescent guest, I was entertained far beyond the call of duty, with acts of lavishness intransigent and ineluctable as the commands of a pharaoh.

The widow spoke little, for it was enough (she said) to make her my friend, that I had been a friend of her husband's. Of our subversive plots she knew nothing, or wished to know nothing. One evening, however, on the pretext that otherwise they would have ended up on the fire, she presented me with a sheaf of secret papers, with lists of names and documents in the hand of *God the Father*, which, if they had come to light, would have turned the whole kingdom topsy-turvy. After which she left me to recover gradually, taking no notice of me except at mealtimes, and otherwise gliding by in silence, slender and erect, a huge bunch of keys at her belt, performing her daily round of the innumerable rooms of the house. Moving meticulously from one to the other, here passing a fingertip over a piece of mahogany or a window pane neglectfully unpolished, there lighting on a couple of maids idling on the floor with their legs asprawl. Slender, erect. Nearer forty years old than thirty, but with virginal blushes, as when I asked her had she no other children, and she was forced to concede that not even this boy was hers, but by a deceased first wife. Restless, grave, imperious, timid . . . Every day I added a further attribute, without being able to make them add up to a plausible total. In the manner of a painter painting a portrait who, filling in now the cheekbone, now the nose, and now the chin, feels he has rendered each feature to perfection, but fails to find upon the canvas the likeness he sought after. Severe with the youngster, although in a few years' time (an event joyfully anticipated by the servants), she would have by the terms of the Will to hand over to him the government of the duchy.

The room I was occupying was indeed on loan from him, and adjacent to that other, the grand bed-chamber of the duchess. Nor was she the least concerned if, more mornings than one, in the crack between the two leaves of the door, I caught a glimpse of her clad in nothing but billowing silks which wafted hither and thither as she walked, revealing a radiance of firm flesh trimmed with a patch of black fleece, as she made her leisurely way to the bath-house.

I was inclined to think that she would have done well not

124

to show herself to me thus defenceless, but I put aside the thought as I observed her demureness throughout the rest of the day. There was also, to rein me in, the way she smelt: a natural odour which her ablutions, far from diminishing, seemed to accentuate, an odour of quince and raisins, sweetish and in the last analysis almost aggressive.

A curious woman, indeed; but my curiosity was still further aroused by the resentment she bore towards the youngster, a pale, ardent adolescent who in the intervals between bouts of malaria revealed himself as a tireless walker. Scarcely was I back on my feet again than he set himself up as my companion on rambles through the surrounding woods and fields, which served to occupy many a long hour. A companion, I say, though still more of an adoring and faithful servant, always at my heels.

It was through him that I first learnt the ecstasies of idleness, if such I may call them: the gyrations of a spinning-top, soporific, monotonous, unending. Everything around it at a standstill, the illusion of a breakdown in time. Call to mind, will you, the fairy-tale of the Sleeping Beauty, the courtiers whom the spell has taken unawares, one with a knee poised in the jigging of a country dance, another with a goblet of wine at his lips, yet another with a half-sniffed pinch of snuff . . . Each one caught in an act of candour or of lewdness, in a marmorial, unalterable grimace or laugh. Just such was I at that time. Although, as I have said, I walked much and looked about me unremittingly, always with that same radiant doltishness with which, from the stony sockets of their eyes, statues in the park gaze before them at some long-lost objective. I felt no emotions, I gave no tongue, every passion now reduced to the chrysalis of itself, barely warmed with a forgotten warmth such as keeps snakes alive in their winter quarters. Life? Ah no; but death neither, nor sleep. A phantom instead, twixt sleep and waking, a sluggishness, a dead calm of the blood, with minimal lappings of waves breaking soundless upon the rocks of consciousness. Such was the state of affairs. Whatever I did, or thought, or said, seemed to come on tiptoe from a long-distant daydream. In all this I was aided by Amabile – the "Gentle One". For such was his name. First and foremost by his silence; then by his animal skill in relishing the minutest detail, whether it be a passing cloud or a sniff of wind in the offing, a couple of apple cores at the foot of an apple tree – living proof that indeed this was the Garden of Eden . . .

He had a miraculous sense of hearing, which registered the most inaudible music of the earth, the air, the waters: the plip of a twig into the bottom of a well, the rustle of the grass sprouting between the stones of a threshing-floor . . . It was his most precious toy, that ear of his. And he taught me to use my own ears; and other games he taught me, which in my headlong childhood I had neglected, or since forgotten. I was, despite being so much older, put in the position of a child yearning for instruction from the example of an elder brother, however much his own feelings and attitudes towards myself remained those of a slave. Still more, perhaps, of a fanatic possessed by love. For it has to be said that he adored me. When I had only just awakened from a siesta, I would see him in the sandy soil of the vineyards, seeking out the imprint of my limbs and laying himself down therein, as if he found in that warm mould the very effigy of himself. Moreover he copied my mannerisms, the way I have of fingering the cleft in my chin when surprised by someone's unexpected kindness, or of slowly smoothing my hair when I have turned a neat phrase . . . He was in love with me. Or rather, he yearned to be me. Which is, perhaps, the most instantaneous and absolute characteristic of love.

He, in any case, in his desire for love was scarcely to be satisfied with the absolute. He wanted more, even though he knew not what. He had no notion of pleasure, of the very existence of pleasure. So much was obvious to me. By this I do not mean to say that pleasure is the absolute, but only that it is a luxury which his mind and body rejected, convinced of its insufficiency. With the result that he had lived sixteen years with no delights except from books; without having known his mother, dead in childbirth; without knowing a father except for a Sunday kiss bristly with damp moustaches; nothing of his stepmother, save the odour which heralded her from afar, well in advance of the padding of her silken slippers.

Deprived of contemporaries, attended only by obsequious tutors and a staff of rustic servants, Amabile had fed upon the pitch and toss of his malarial fevers in the same way – between calm and rapture – as we healthy people watch the alternation of light and darkness.

It was therefore an upheaval for him to come across me, with my foreign-sounding speech, come from a distant star to upset the syllabary of his days. After so many solitary duels and deaf-mute discussions with his paladin puppets, I was the first-comer with whom he could play. For my part, having been always a townsman and having never until then had dealings with the thousand arcane and minuscule monsters of a country summer, I could scarcely believe it when with his help I began to become familiar with sand-fly or cockroach, may-fly and tarantula, skylark and viper . . . presences which he was aware of without even seeing them, just as he imperturbably discovered underground veins of water simply by gripping a forked stick. Now and again he would put a finger to his lips and take me by the hand. In silence, tiptoeing from tussock to tussock, without causing alarm or feeling any fear ourselves, we would gaze down each time upon some new creature in the intimacy of its lair. He maintained he had singled out and distinguished its vibrations among the orchestra of

127

sylvan voices, and felt every nerve tremble from his toes to his fingertips. In similar manner he discerned the whisper of buried springs perhaps three hundred feet below ground.

On certain evenings he took me to the river. Donna Matilda spied on us from aloft, assuming that it was hers, that black chignon which swiftly vanished from the window. We went down by a path through overarching green canes, forcing our way with elbows, knives and knees, guided by the sound of the stream, ever closer and more friendly. A-shiver at the first touch of chill, the bare foot declined to enter, preferring to rest upon a water-worn stone much as a castaway reaches safety on a rock. From here we had no further reason to move: we could scoop out the fish with our hands . . .

On our return, even as we were climbing the stairs, unfailingly we were assailed at one and the same time by the waltz-tune of *Printemps au bois* and the odour of the duchess, whose fingers wore themselves out on the keyboard of a recalcitrant pianola. She left off when she saw us enter, passed her tongue over her parched lips, and placed her hands palm uppermost in her lap. A technique for having her palms admired, for there was not a line nor a wrinkle in them. A peculiarity of which I know of no other example, and which constantly seemed to me ominous, and in some way connected with witchcraft. Of the witch she also had about her that mocking slant of the eye, and a way of swinging her whole body from the hips, which gave her gait a disharmony that both limped and took wing. I was forced to a still deeper conviction on the night when, chancing to wake, outside the bolted door I sensed a hidden presence from a sigh or a breath which did not match my own. I had only to show signs of getting up, thereby making the bed creak, but swift soft footsteps faded away along the labyrinthine corridors . . .

The following morning, opening the door with effort on account of an obstruction on the other side, I found a cock with its legs tied together and its eyes torn out, struggling and bleeding and pitifully encumbering the threshold. Was this witchcraft? . . . I laughed the thought off. I preferred to think of it as a figure of speech or rhetorical metaphor for my life, although I had no idea what the unknown author of the deed wished to accuse me of.

I ought to have given the matter more thought, but I had no wish to. Such was the lake of gold and of enjoyable tranquillity in which with broad strokes I swam. Nor would there be anything more to add concerning this my experiment in serenity had it not been twisted to end in horror, as I will now relate.

A messenger from the capital came to seek me out. News had arrived there of the duke's death, and they did not understand my delay in returning. Those were the early days of the conspiracy, pleasantly impetuous, when heroism did not tolerate half-measures or holidays. *God the Father* in person (I had not yet been admitted to his acquaintance, though I received periodical and personal commands from him) had sent word that I was needed, that vast exploits were afoot on the Continent. I now know that he was deluding himself, that he had sketched a characteristic castle-in-the-air between one game of lansquenet and the next; as so often in the twenty years that followed, in an hallucination of vain hopes and self-deception: indefatigable struggles of an Ixion, similar to the one which is today leading us to the scaffold. I did not, however, hesitate to obey. Just as even now I do not hesitate, convinced as I am that any failure whatsoever serves to water the seeds of success; and that to nourish our cause it may be better to die than to live. In me, in any case, caution and imprudence have always been one and the same thing, nor have I ever relinquished the impossible on the feeble grounds that it was, in point of fact, impossible. So one evening, while we were sitting peacefully in the open air enjoying the smell of the earth after a passing storm, all of a sudden I announced my departure.

We were on the terrace, close by a balustrade between the columns of which one glimpsed fragments of tenebrous valley, and the weaving of torches therein; snail-hunters, perhaps, searching along the stone walls. A coolness arose from the earth like a moistened handkerchief caressing our limbs. The silence had such a sweetness to it as to be almost intolerable.

This I broke by announcing my imminent departure, and it was as if I had struck them with an axe. Seconds later the duchess burst into a fit of tears that staggered me: Oh, by all means! High time I got away! Already too long, this month which she and Amabile had robbed from my life and bestowed on their own . . .

Words totally unexpected, from her lips; the only sign of a fervour which, plain enough in the boy, there had been nothing to induce me to imagine existed also in her, concealed as it was behind the mask of enforced hospitality.

I took her hand in mine, and hers was scorching, trembling, a firebrand from a forge, of such contagious love-force that a rush of blood struck me at the nape of the neck, such an artless desire to possess her that it caused me in turn to tremble from head to foot.

The lad was too upset to be aware of anyone else's distress. He began to eat compulsively, he also weeping copious tears.

Regaining my composure, I rose to my feet, and without looking back retired to my bedroom, where later on I heard the echoes of a mysterious altercation.

My departure was arranged for the following Sunday, and they both intended to accompany me, she driving a two-in-hand and the boy on horseback as far as the coast where, God willing, I would take ship.

Preparations for departure were artfully prolonged, and I

myself gladly fell in with these postponements, after the manner of a tenant who with the passing of the years has become one with the very fabric of the place, and says to himself on his departure that some day or other he will return.

But I was not, on this account, less anxious to be off, as I always am when, having once decided to make a move, the place in which I still am, and the hours still to run, seem to me the mere leftovers of the present; a mere effigy of life which has to be done away with and buried as soon as possible. It was in this state of mind that I set out.

It was one of those crystal-clear days that in mid-August, here in the South, suddenly wedge themselves between two Moorish dogdays, and with their limpid air foretell the coming of autumn; though not stamped with that shadow of tender, piercing grief that will come later, with the first whistlings of the north wind through the loose boards of attics and in the hollows of trees.

Matilda drove the two-in-hand, Amabile in the saddle brought up the rear, with an air so downcast and adult that he looked like a father escorting his own son's funeral exequies. Nor am I exaggerating, for I noticed that to the mourning band already sewn to his lapel in memory of the deceased duke he had added another in honour of my symbolic death. Even the fact that the two of them had rejected an escort of postillions and servitors confirmed the personal and funebral significance of that farewell.

We had already passed the turning at Centorbi when I was startled by a cry. The duchess had let go the reins and was staring at her bare hands.

"I've lost it! I've lost it!" she shrieked out, brandishing a finger and all but poking it into the face of her stepson, who had drawn up beside her, with a gesture that might have seemed a threat but was in fact nothing other than a desperate supplication.

131

"Go back and search for it!" she implored. "It must have come off there at the bends at Biddini, when I gave a sharp tug at the reins. We will wait for you in the shed by the tarn."

The lad cast her a strange look, then wheeled his horse around and made off.

"Don't dare come back without the ring!" she shouted after him. Then she stepped down from the carriage and started off towards the copse of cork-oaks, in the middle of which was the tarn.

The "tarn" was in fact a circular irrigation lake, beside which stood a shack which might have been a stable, or else a shelter for farm workers. Around us was an assembly of cork-oaks with the stern expression of spectators, making a theatre of the place and reducing our every act to the level of stage business.

All of you know my love of the opera. I had scarcely plucked a green spray to bedizen my hat, as in the last Act of *Fra Diavolo*, when the fact corroborated the fantasy. The duchess had already taken herself off to the shelter, while I, who had lingered behind for a drink, was on my knees and lowering my lips to the water, when between eyelids half-closed in anticipation of that imminent cool draught I seemed to discern that the sun had veiled himself with a strange vapour.

When I opened them fully to see what was afoot, I saw another reflection beside my own, as bearded as mine was clean-shaven, saw it clearer and clearer as the ripples made in the water by my hands little by little stilled themselves.

No need to turn round: the prick of a knife-blade in my ribs informed me that this, for me, was a crucial moment.

"I am Salibba," said a voice, and it was enough.

This Salibba was the most famous bandit in the duchy. They said of him that he ate the flesh of his enemies raw.

I turned my head to look at him now: a massive beard, a

low forehead beneath his broad-brimmed, conical hat, wolfish teeth between leering lips, huge protruding ears as mobile as an extra pair of hands. He had crept up behind me with the tread of a phantom, but now he pushed me vociferously in front of him, not without first binding my wrists with a length of stout cord, guffawing all the while. Then, with a jack-knife jabbing into my ribs, he forced me into the shack. Unaware of events, when she saw us enter Matilda shrieked. A single cry, as of an animal caught in a snare. Then she collapsed into a corner of the stable, her face clenched tight as a fist. He coughed out his guffaw, gave my arms a further twist of the rope, and lashed me to an upright in the middle of the shed. He was still laughing as he seized hold of the woman and thrust her onto her back in the straw.

I heard the rasp of her dress as it ripped, and two or three buttons bounce onto the beaten earth floor. Her breasts, burgeoning forth, appeared more than usually disparate in size, for the left one was that of a young girl, like the Sicilian almond cakes they call "nun's breasts", while the other was almost obese, with a nipple so dark as to make one think of a shield with a rusted boss. Between the two glittered a gem, which fell soundlessly onto the sundered garment lying limply about her. It was a jewel I recognized with a sense of astonished jubilation – it was the ring that would be sought for in vain, the unlost diamond . . .

So she had hidden it away simply to be alone with me! This realization, even more than her body, now naked to the full, overwhelmed me and fired desire in me. Even though I was condemned to be present, a maddened witness to someone else's paroxysms.

But at this point, almost as if he had read my thoughts, Salibba seemed to recall my presence. He disentangled the speechless, inert woman from the heap of garments, and one of these he flung over my head, blinding me on the instant, like the cock of ill omen. After that I saw nothing more, I made nothing out, save at first the hoarse grunts of the man, and later another voice in unison, a whimper on the edge of words; the litany, the carnal imprecations of a woman beside herself, praying as a goad to incite herself to pleasure.

When, with a jerk of the head, I succeeded in procuring a spyhole through the folds of the garment, I caught a glimpse of the man – already broken away and standing on the threshold, making sure that no one was coming – and of the woman sprawled in the bed of straw. I was struck above all by her lips, defibrated by kisses, half open in the expectation of more, and as red as a whiplash in the pallor of her face. Tragic and sated, her eyes sought heaven knows what in the rafters, and her whole body was as if rapt by some turbid saintly martyrdom.

Very soon the man broke off his vigilance. She thereupon, with a gesture of the head, beckoned him back, and he fell upon her again, and I saw him thrust into her for the second time. Both of them silent this time, committed to working together, as if sawing a tree-trunk, hammering antiphonally on an anvil, rowing a boat . . . A serious job, worth sweating over . . .

I did not at first notice the entry of Amabile. Some second thoughts, some suspicion or foreboding, must have made him turn back. He instantly hurled himself upon the brigand, pummelling his back with small fists.

"Get out of here, boy!" I tried to shout through the gag of the garment, but he, far from hearing me, was not even aware of my presence.

Salibba slowly extricated himself, and yet it was not he but the woman, on her feet at the same moment, who slapped Amabile in the face. He reeled for an instant, and then, never taking his eyes off hers, backed to the doorway and disappeared. Nor did Salibba linger for long. A flash and a snap of his wolfish teeth was his manner of bidding farewell.

The woman took her time before untying me. First she dressed herself with the motions of a sleepwalker, lazily and methodically. When we left the shed Amabile's horse was drinking at the tarn, and the saddle was empty. Wherever the boy was, he had fled away on foot.

We went fruitlessly calling for him down towards the river. There at last we saw him. He was sitting perched on a rock overhanging the brink, his feet dangling in the void. Only at the third cry, "Amabile, Amabile!" did he react. But merely to stare at us unseeingly, stamped on his features both loathing and some kind of malevolent exultation. As if he was thinking, before he leapt, that we would forever carry that look implanted in our hearts like a dagger.

We had a struggle to clamber down the escarpment through the weeds and the wilderness before we could gather up his body from the dry river bed, where it lay with the head askew, the neck snapped by a boulder. In his plummet his shoulder had come to rest in a hollow in the ground, mimicking the grace with which each night he found the shape of his sleep in his bed and his pillow. Face hidden, pressed into the gravel. Under one leg swarmed the inmates of an ants' nest disturbed, though not destroyed, by the impact. All around was a vasty silence. His arms were spread like wings.

TWELVE

Throw of the Dice

The poet fell silent, and Brother Cirillo spoke.

"Well, well, well!" he exclaimed, and seemed about to launch into a discourse, but pulled himself up.

So Saglimbeni pressed him, saying "What do you think of my story?"

"That's soon said," answered the friar. "It's a sham. And you, in all honesty, claimed that right from the very start. Though in fact you only twisted the ending – the cheat is at the end."

"I doff my cap to you, sir," smirked Saglimbeni. "However, tell me something: how did you catch me out? Come now, tell me."

"There were only two of you there in the shed, not three," explained Brother Cirillo in easy tones. "You yourself are the man whom the boy found riding the woman. He would never have killed himself out of jealousy of a bandit. Only from disenchantment with you."

"And what about Salibba?" enquired the others.

"Salibba never existed," the friar went on to explain. "He's a scapegoat on whom Saglimbeni unloads his remorse."

"You must admit it was a fine name for a brigand," smiled the poet. "And anyway, I'll have you know my story can take another turn and end on a happier note. That an ample nine months after the death of the duke, the duchess gave birth to a baby boy, a praiseworthy effort on the old man's part, they said, to keep the name alive after his demise. Almost as if he foresaw the premature decease of Amabile. And that since then Donna Matilda, now plump and placid, has governed the immense duchy on behalf of the new heir. To her husband and to her stepson she brings flowers every week, and sheds her heartfelt tears upon their graves."

"Right," said the soldier, who seemed to have taken it on himself to play sentry to the passing of time. "It may be because, being a poet, you talk more fluently than the rest of us, but you certainly discharged your obligation in less time; for though the hour draws nigh, it is not yet five o'clock."

He crossed to the window-embrasure, where a first flake of light was astir, more dream, more mirage than true light.

"It's coming along. Yes, yes, it's coming along," he muttered as he returned to his seat. And they realized that he was speaking not of the day but of the scaffold, now completely fitted out, including the wooden railing and the steps, at the foot of which could be seen Smiriglio, teetering on a stool and imparting his last orders to the workmen.

The baron then turned to the poet, trying to keep up the conversation, saying "That fellow Byron you referred to before, I read nothing else when I was a young man. And again in these last few months it has occurred to me to make a comparison between the position of the three prisoners in the cells below lake-level at Chillon, chained in such a way as not to be able to see each other, and our situation up here, which in all truth is a mite less ferocious. Contrariwise, I am intrigued by another passage from the same poem. In which the survivor, released from prison, admits:

> . . . even I
> Regained my freedom with a sigh.

O lamentable sigh, O pregnant admission! Not only with regard to our own destiny, but to that of the peoples in general . . ."

"I fail to follow you," said Narcissus.

"And yet," said the baron, "it is a question which might well have concerned you more than others, and which can be expressed in this manner: what boots it to shed one's blood for people so in love with their chains that they weep to be free of them? Until now I always thought that only lovers loved their shackles . . ."

"Whereas you now realize," put in the friar, "that to a long-time slave the surprise of freedom can inflict an all but intolerable fit of vertigo."

"Do you mean to say . . ." Here the soldier rose to his feet again, almost menacingly this time. "Do you mean to say that to the millions of men to whom we are sacrificing our heads, the gift we are giving them, this gift of liberty, might appear, if not positively odious, at least irksome? Is this your meaning?"

"Exactly that." The baron spoke without looking up. "And this doubt is more thorny than it seems to be. Because it follows that, since our death is useless, we might as well save our lives, even on the most iniquitous terms."

"Ah, you too are tempted to play Judas!" murmured the boy, appearing simultaneously both relieved and disconsolate. "Don't you see," he added to the others, "how these ups and downs which we have been telling each other about, be they imaginary, probable, or perfectly true, may very easily be used as pretexts or inducements to surrender . . . So I am not the only one to be shaking in his boots! Although, I swear I quake solely within my conscience, without any romanticizing with sighs and tears about the destinies of the human race. My choice is to be made in the down-to-earth terms of whether to betray or not to betray, whether to live or die . . .

And it is a challenge to myself, a throw of the dice in which the stake is honour. And the arbiter is God."

Agesilaos cleared his throat.

"I'm not one for quibbling," he began. "I am a soldier. But one thing I do see clearly: that we started off on the supposition of narrating some joyful thing so as to cherish it in our mind's eye until the end; or else for the last time, in words, to travel outside these walls; or else again, as a pastime, a confession, an insight into ourselves . . . But it seems to me that on the contrary each of us is bringing up some extraneous, some obscene memory, and, without admitting it, nursing it in his bosom. In a word, if I must be honest, I am afraid that here we are furtively eyeing and comparing four examples of cowardice, my own not excluded."

There fell a painful silence, interrupted at length by Brother Cirillo, who had been listening with a merry glint in what could be seen of his eyes through a fissure in the rags and clots of dried blood.

"I," he said, "since I do not know that name, do not have to confess it, and am therefore above suspicion. There is no possible pardon for my misdeeds, or any way to save my head. One thing, however, I can say to you from this position of neutrality: that you are not the first, as perhaps you are priding yourselves on being, to be forced to choose between two ultimate modes of conduct. And I am surprised at you, Agesilaos, who have studied theology, and ought not to be ignorant of the moral doctrine of the Loyolites, according to whose teaching, when the reasons working towards freedom are more plausible and in evidence than what appears to be one's duty, then it is lawful to act counter to that duty . . ."

"Even if someone is bound to die for it?" asked the soldier, with set lips.

"Fie on you! Four lives on one side of the scale are four times weightier than the one on the other."

"One life at present, perhaps, but thousands and thousands in the future. Apart from the wellbeing of the peoples, from civic trust . . ."

Brother Cirillo shrugged.

"And hey nonny no!" said he. "Such things are a load of balderdash not worth a single scruple of your blood. And you know it too, since the nearer the moment of your sacrifice approaches the more you feel the throb of the lifeblood in your veins, and the more deflated and vacuous appears that miasma of high-sounding prattle. That is why, as the scales tip this way and that, I see you so bewildered . . ."

"We might toss up for it," suggested the poet. "If it's heads, then we'll talk, and keep our heads on. If it's tails, then we'll go to the scaffold with our tails up, but our lips sealed." And then, more seriously, "These see-sawings of will-power, I realize why they come to vex us – we who until a little while ago were so grave and so sure of ourselves. The fact is that death is such an exceptional event as to dismay anyone, when he sniffs it from really close to. But it is also true that we make more of it than it is worth, simply because we are dazzled by fancies; much as, in the timorous eye of the traveller, bushes in the undergrowth in the shades of night take on the shapes of giants."

"With which the matter returns to the point of departure," insisted the friar obstinately. "Of how much your death is or is not beneficial to your Cause. This is the leap of Leucas."

"For my part," said the baron, "I cannot help thinking of the problem set to Pascal by the Chevalier de Méré, that of how the stakes should be divided among the players if they are obliged to abandon the game while one of their number is at an advantage . . ."

"What's that got to do with it?" It was always Narcissus who asked the most ingenuous questions.

"Simply that the game interrupted today is the game of

our lives, and that it is up to us to apportion the gains and losses according to Pascal's calculations of probability . . ."

"The comparison is forced," protested Saglimbeni. "I myself, though willing to hold with Pascal, would prefer to draw a lesson from his famous principle, that the force exerted: on an enclosed liquid presses equally on all other points. That, if we accept our blood to be a liquid, and I mean the blood we are about to shed, it follows . . ."

"I would remind you that it is five o'clock," said the soldier.

"And I, that it is time to keep our promise. We have talked it over with the most brazen permissiveness, but now let each of us be alone with himself for a minute, and decide."

Thus saying, the baron rose, and the other three did likewise. He remained on his feet, eyes closed, while Brother Cirillo, still recumbent on his bunk, scrutinized them each in turn. A short time passed, and then they trooped up to the table that might turn them King's evidence, where Ingafù with a firm hand was the first to pen a line on a blank sheet and thrust it through the slit. The others followed suit calmly, or so it appeared, though Narcissus (or so it appeared) with an air of desperation.

"Now that that's over and done with," said the baron gravely, "there only remains your turn, Brother Cirillo. Afterwards . . . hap what may.

THIRTEEN

Diabolus ex Machina

"No, I will not tell you the story of my life," said Brother Cirillo. "You would either not listen at all or listen with half an ear. More often than once, in the last minute or so, I have seen you staring at that little box on the table, in which you have deposited your fate. And wondering the while, I suppose, whether the Mouth of Truth will speak. And if so, with whose voice? And if not, how advantageous was it to stay silent?

"As for the tales you have told, what shall I say? Possibly it was not a good idea of mine to suggest a nocturnal *Decameron* of this sort, since the result has been a torment to each and every one of you, stripping you totally naked in the bleakness of your reasonings. The fact is that, whichever way each of you has this moment solved the dilemma, and become an informer or otherwise, all of you, be it only for a moment and in the secrecy of your hearts, have been disloyal. And if you die, you will die dissatisfied with yourselves, with your life and with your death. I know that yesterday you rejected the prison chaplain and the comforts of religion. Was it worth it, if you were then going to confess to an unknown sinner, an apostate and a highwayman?"

There was a ring in his voice of such unexpectedly mocking but at the same time heroic timbre that the four friends were astonished by it. Not least because from the tangle of rags which, in the first light already striking through the window, seemed grotesquely torn away at the neck, there showed one of those bloody bundles in which foetuses are concealed before being deposited in the rubbish.

The voice went on: "It is not my task to set myself up as your third judge, after the profane synedrion which condemned you and the divine one which is about to condemn you. But one thing is certain: that however much I might have pretended to the contrary, you have all revealed yourselves in my eyes as either evil, or weak, or foolish – tiny souls a-shiver in a tinsel splendour. You for a start, you obsessive castrator and parricide; you next, seducer of widows and orphans; you sir, a Cain disguised as an Abel; and finally you, amorous Narcissus, unworthy to bear a name denoting such tragic and exclusive solitude . . .

"Oh, truly I have felt myself your guardian devil during this night of marvels, the most sumptuous in all my life, playing hide-and-seek with your boastings and fears . . . And even flattering you a little (now I can say it) to egg you on to perform, while I set myself up as both creator and spectator. For I have exploited you in two contrary ways, now craftily manipulating your strings, now sitting in silence to relish your play-acting; now your adversary, now your conniver, without ever revealing to you the nature of what I truly was – the puppeteer of each and every one of you . . . But in the depths of my soul consistently enraged to hear you, on the very doorstep of the dark, confusing the great questions, of God, evil, death, with the little ones, such as king, Constitution, happiness, deliverance, decorum . . ."

"You wish to make laughing stock of all our doings," protested the soldier wrathfully. But Saglimbeni nailed him with a gesture.

"Let him have his say. There's some method in his madness . . ."

In the meantime the light had boldened, and long grey

quiffs of it hung from the grating. A pattering murmur revealed that it had started to rain again, and that the morn was destined to be sunless.

"Pray continue, I am interested," said the baron, as from the furthest depths of the dungeon, though muffled by distance, they heard the lunatic cackle his habitual cock-a-doodle-doo to the stone walls.

"St Peter did not wait to hear the cock crow," commented the friar. "Perhaps one of you has done likewise . . ."

The baron shrugged. "You will soon see, when the ballot-box is unsealed. In the meanwhile, since you despise us so greatly, and chide us so much for our stories, and do not intend to tell us yours, then hold your tongue and nod off, if you can."

"Oh, no!" protested Narcissus. "We are in no position to take offence. And the silence would be intolerable, while we wait for the Governor. Speak on, I beg of you; and if not your history from beginning to end, then tell us some little thing about yourself."

Cirillo calmed down, like a soothed child placated.

"On those terms, yes. I know, in any case, that I am speaking to ears that I can trust, because soon to be the deafest, the most discreet in the world . . . Small chance that I am unknown to you. You will have read about me a thousand times at every street corner, on proclamations promising sacks of gold in return for my head or the seizure of my person. And you will have read that I am an old man of seventy, and that the title of Brother was bestowed on me for my likeness to Fra Diavolo of yore, but perhaps even more on account of my craving for pious practices, which I imbibed at my mother's breast. Never did I fail in observation of them, even in the most calamitous predicaments; not even when I found myself most bitterly at variance with the Heavens. So that it was no rare thing for me to be seen on my knees, with the hands I had joined in prayer still besmirched with blood.

"How I became a brigand is on the tongues of the whole populace, and has even been made a ballad of. This tells of how I as a young man, rich and studious, held to be an excellent philosopher in Naples, a city not lacking in such persons, came to marry the lovely Ninfa Carafa. That within the year I surprised her in the arms of the most notorious gallant at court, and ran them both through with cold steel. How I fled to the mountains and joined the gang of the Vardarelli brothers, eager for the boldest excesses of body and spirit, and how on their death I made myself the chief of a makeshift rabble armed with axes and hatchets, and roved throughout the country. A colleague of yours, though in grosser and more excessive ways, yet with the selfsame purpose of subverting, from the bottom up, the flourishing régime of the kingdom.

"This, roughly speaking, is what is sung of me, and though things may well have been otherwise, I have no wish to disclose anything further. My career is certainly, in the eyes of the world, that of an impenitent, but I do not ask for absolution, because I absolve myself. For every act of mine over the last forty years has been caused by the one before, by irresistible force, as a boulder falls from the top of a long, steep mountain slope, and willy-nilly cannot come to rest, unless it be received into some valley, where the very levelness of the place should check its course. As in an hour's time will happen to us, and to the course we have run. But not before I have declaimed against the injustice of being born at all. The same which you, Agesilaos, in your confusion punished in your father. And also the other, greater injustice, of neither you nor I nor any one of us having a solid, imperturbable, responsible 'I' of his own. For my own life, no less than yours, my brethren and antagonists, has been naught but a steady flow of multiple perceptions within a multiple self . . . And it may be that evening after evening I implored God for nothing else than to be able to rest secure at last in the name Cirillo, in the lonesome, incomparable name of Cirillo, rather than to feel both my name and my fate leaking out on all sides like water through a sieve. Thus my most ferocious bloodbaths were aimed at this and this alone: to convince myself that I existed by means of the pain of another, inflicted by me. Whereas now I come to the pass, as do you all. My fate has been the selfsame fate as yours, for I have been listening to you, some more some less, falling into the same shiftings and shadow-play, and exchanges of personality and blindman's-buff, which has been the warp and the weft of my own life. We resemble, all of us together, the rotting shreds of a dismembered cartulary. Small-part actors, you and I are, in an endless sham. Mummers in a weird and an odious misunderstanding . . ."

"Do you mean to say," protested Narcissus, "that our high-minded vigil is nothing but a charade?"

The baron, seemingly unmoved by this remark, began, "My erstwhile friend, Baron Pasquale Galluppi, would have voiced these folderols better than we can. Of him I remember that as we were walking together he told me about certain Greek prisoners shut up in a cavern from birth, who saw only shadows on the wall, and mistook them for things real. But I hear that he has died, Galluppi has . . ."

"The truth, how can one ever know it?" Saglimbeni began to sing to himself, and proceeded to explain, "Rossini, *Opportunity Makes the Thief*, Berenice's aria . . ."

Brother Cirillo shook his head, turning to the baron.

"Oh, I had no desire to make a philosophic discourse," he said. "I wished only to express what an unstable alloy of a man I am, and how humbly I pray to God that he may shortly gather me in and annihilate me in His sole, unique countenance . . ."

Saglimbeni did not give up. He seemed set on exorcizing fear with chatter.

"Did you happen to hear that piece of doggerel I wrote years ago, which has to do with alloys?" And he declaimed,

> "Vainly will you spend your time
> And vainly fight your battles
> If you try to make an alloy
> Of your arse and stinging nettles."

But thereupon the baron: "You were not even three years old when that ruffianly rubbish was going round the streets."

And the poet spoke no more.

"Another hour," said Agesilaos, hearing the changing of the guard. "It's six o'clock." And he withdrew into his thoughts.

"Your arse and stinging nettles!" The friar laughed an ambiguous laugh. "Well, as in that lewd rhyme, in my person four or five incompatible elements attempt in vain to form an alloy: the bigot and the play-actor, the God-fearing man and the murderer; sometimes even the apostle of the common people . . . I am more unaccountable to myself than is the unknown *God the Father* to the members of your conspiracy."

"I wonder if at this moment he fears we are traitors," murmured the baron, half closing his eyes. And thereupon seemed to drift off who knows where.

"Could he not, in the meantime, just as a precaution, move to a place of safety?" the friar asked Narcissus in an undertone.

The lad was not reticent: "He can't, not where *he* is! He would create a scandal if he disappeared from public."

"Naturally," said the friar. "At court every absence is noticed . . ." And seeing Narcissus nod, he continued: "Unless, as is obligatory, he asks leave from the king to travel abroad. Or if not from the king himself, from the king's brother . . ."

147

By this time Narcissus alone was heeding him. The rest sat lifeless, staring straight ahead, suddenly prostrated by some stupor, some drowsiness.

"Yes, the king's brother," continued the friar; and his voice was like the coaxing murmur of some fount of clear water. "He who is so fond of travelling and never begrudges an audience . . ."

"Who, the Count of Syracuse?" cried the young man. Then, impulsively, "That would be easy indeed, as easy as winking. It would be enough for *God the Father* to request an audience from his own looking glass . . ."

And he drew his lips into a sardonic smile – lips weary and chapped by wakefulness and fasting. Strange, how he was growing older and uglier by the minute.

"*God the Father* request an audience from the Count of Syracuse!" he repeated, nudging his companions who sat shoulder to shoulder on the one bed, as lifeless and mindless as sentinels at the Holy Sepulchre.

"Of course," laughed the friar. "How could he request an audience from himself?" And Narcissus laughed with him. But only for an instant, while the others had no time to pull themselves together before they heard the friar cry out in triumph:

"So my lad! Your laughter is proof enough. I have got the better of you, and need you no more!"

His voice suddenly took on a different timbre, but one that was somehow familiar to the ears of the prisoners, who started back to life on seeing the friar leap to his feet with a nimbleness they could scarcely credit, stride to the door, and knock thrice upon it with imperative knuckles.

The same instant that an armed guard entered and took up position in the corners of the room, there flashed on the memories of the four men the secret of that voice. But the friar, with swift movements, was already freeing his head of the spurious dressings – a bushy wig, a kind of toupee, fell at his feet along with the last of the bandages, revealing a sweaty grey head emerging from the pomades of his make-up and, with its stony albumen, one blind eye. Only then, blenching with a start, did the student, the baron, the soldier, the poet, recognize beneath the loosened wrappings and the cast-off linens the Governor's familiar ugly mug.

"Sparafucile!" they exclaimed in chorus. Nor could one tell, to look at them, whether it was consternation or relief that caused their eyes to glitter and their voices to quiver.

From the folds of his clothing Sparafucile drew out a black patch, with which he covered his blind eye, and subsequently a small key to unlock the iron box. Silence reigned in the cell. The soldiers had relit the flares in the brackets, although there was no difficulty now in seeing, and the flames paled against the first harsh light of day. Slowly Sparafucile unlocked the casket, drew out the papers, weighed them between finger and thumb.

"I am not obliged to be held to it," he said, "now that I know the name of the hydra, but in virtue of an unwritten law my promise stands. If one of you has voluntarily confessed, your lives will all be saved."

He crossed to the window and set himself to read with his one good eye.

After a little he remarked, "I should have regretted it if anyone had in fact turned informer, thus rendering my exploit fruitless and futile."

Then, in a duller tone: "I can bequeath you scarcely an hour to preen yourselves over these foul oaths." And he held aloft the paper slips. "A single hour to spend in mutual congratulation. But nourish no hopes that *these* will survive or go down in history."

And so saying he tore them to shreds.

"All I wrote was *merde*," said the baron placidly. "Which, after all, was a plagiarism."

Sparafucile let out a guffaw.

"I rejoice," he said, "because I was always convinced of your unbridled folly and, as you have seen, to put you to rout I have followed the most artful and devious courses. Now that I know where the hydra lurks, at the very foot of the throne, no more is needed for the moment but to lop off the nearest tentacles and consign them to the sea, where yesterday the genuine Brother Cirillo preceded you."

Of a sudden he fell silent. After a night of truce the rat had made its presence felt inside his skull, albeit so benignly as to make him think it must be sending signals of peace and of farewell; as at the end of a storm a tardy drop strikes the forehead, or as the arrow of a fleeing Parthian falls harmless at our feet. He smoothed his palms up over his temples, almost as if these were the cheeks of a son in need of consolation. Then, out loud to himself, with confidence: "Something shall be managed," he said.

Falling of a sudden into despondency, he turned to the four men: "Let us go, then, you to die, I to live. God knows whose fate is the worse."

Narcissus muttered, "I'm frightened."

"It's all over," said Agesilaos; and the poet nodded.

But the baron said, "Who knows?"

FOURTEEN

Papers Found on a
Carrier-Pigeon by a Hunter

Last Will and Testament of Consalvo De Ritis

I, the undersigned Consalvo De Ritis, Knight of Putigli-ano, trusting myself to be sound in body, and presuming myself to be of sound mind, in the certain knowledge that I am at the end of my life, establish and appoint my Sovereign the King to be my universal heir, both of my properties and of my movables, of whatsoever nature these may be, which I may leave at the moment of my death, that he may enjoy and dispose of them as his own property, this to be reckoned from the aforesaid moment.

I desire also that my body, having become a cold corpse, be buried in the church of Montecalvario, to which, with the request that it be spent in almsgiving, I bequeath the sum of thirty *denari* in coins of purest gold.

God rest my soul.

Signed: Consalvo De Ritis
Countersigned: Aniello Balestra

Letter to the King of the aforementioned

I, Consalvo De Ritis, Knight of Putigliano, with this explanatory letter accompany my last holographic Will, coun-tersigned informally, as in those testaments which notaries call "mystic", by my orderly Balestra, and entrusted to him so that he may humbly present it in person and lay it at the august feet of Your Majesty.

In the fear, almost the certainty, that this man may meet with an impeditive injury by means of some hostile and jealous hand, I intend to secure a copy to the leg of a carrier pigeon, as is customary with the more confidential dispatches, in the hope that, evading the turbulence of the skies and the traps laid by the keepers of lighthouses, it may escape from the island and attain its goal.

At all events I give a description of the packet, folded in six and sealed with red wax bearing the impression of my arms: a camel drinking at a pool and the legend, *Il me plaît le trouble*. A prophetic motto, chosen by an ancestor almost as a gloss to my own life, since I, like the desert beast, have never drunk from a source that I have not first trampled underfoot and rendered muddy and vile ... For this in part I take nature to task for having burdened me with a temperament at once indecisive and fanatical; and in part these present times: so heterogeneous are they, that every principle wavers and slips from the grasp of the believer. Granted that these garrison officers do not tend to stick to the truth, nevertheless I almost seem to hear them tomorrow, during the requiem Mass, whispering to each other that in recent months they have seen me strange in act and strained in visage, an enthusiastic talker and scribbler of a morning, silent and surly of an evening. Someone will no doubt mutter that I was completely out of my mind ...

Whether rightly or wrongly they criticize me, I ask Your Majesty to be the judge, and this letter the witness. To be sure I have suffered both in body and mind. In body on account of a creature – horsefly? cockroach? sewer rat? – which long ago crept in at the porches of my ear while I was sleeping beneath a summery tree. This by sightless meanderings reached the very centre of my brain, and there it lodged with no further desire to leave it. It grew and grew, encroaching upon every part of my body, becoming so tame that I have named it Mustachio, imagining it to be whiskered, and by such name I call to it, I scold it, I implore it . . . Without knowing whether I am its trusty hidey-hole or the trap it has fallen into. Hence was born this black bile and rage of melancholy, and the black dreams, the bedlam thoughts.

Here we see where disease approaches ethics, and will have no use for leeches, or mustard plasters, or infusions of cherry laurel . . . For, subsequent to the famous death of Baron Ingafù and his associates, and the denouncement made by me of the great intrigue contrived even in the innermost chambers of the realm; and the consequent censorious banishment, with all its commotion and opprobrium, of the Count of Syracuse; although he declared himself to be guiltless of treason; after this I , who had been the instigator and creator of this indictment, began to nurse a doubt that soon poisoned me with bile and has reduced me to such a state that, in order that I may suffer it no more, the sole possible expedient seems to me death.

Your Majesty, having received such information right speedily, is aware of how in the garments of another I insinuated myself into the last vigil of the condemned men and was able to obtain by guile the Open Sesame which uncovered the hidden recesses of the conspiracy. You are not aware, however, of what I confess today, head bowed with shame. Which is, that I corroborated the presumption of guilt with false evidence planted by me, which was, as if by accident, discovered in the hunting-lodge of the accused man. A liberty I had recourse to very unwillingly, but which I deemed necessary, fortifying myself in the adamantine crystal of my own judgement. Had it not been that, thereafter, as I revolved those hours of multiloquence many times over in my mind, a briar patch sprang up in my head, pricking me ever more fiercely as little by little I brought to mind certain winks that passed between the baron and his men, barely perceptible manoeuvres, and various other inklings of deceit. To make myself plainer, my fear is that rather than fooling them, I was myself fooled. That I put on wolf's clothing only to find myself in a den of deadly ferrets. Or were they not perhaps aware from the start of who I was and what I was aiming at? Did they not keep their silence with the sole purpose of instilling into me the name of an innocent man, relying on my being vain enough to think I had elicited it? So I incited Your Majesty, your heir being brought to disrepute by damning evidence, with your own hands to rid yourself of him, thereby conniving to extinguish the dynasty more surely than if I had myself hidden a bomb in a basket of roses . . .

To all this I must add a qualm, which gives me no peace: that it was through my own fault that they discovered me, by revealing that I, in the person of Cirillo, was privy to the secret pardon promised them by Consalvo. It was from that moment on, I recall, that those blackguards began to whisper to each other, to exchange signs, continuing to do so on the very steps of the scaffold, whence they regarded me mockingly, before offering their necks to the blade . . .

What more can I say? That I might have remained even now in tormented silence, if an inquiry conducted both in the kingdom and abroad by my lawyers (*can I trust them, or are they not also emissaries plotting my ruin?*) had not completely opened my eyes and, at the same time, bewildered my mind. Their reports assured me that of the Ingafù twins the one who died in Paris was the elder, not the younger; nor was it from a bullet in the face, but by hanging himself from a tree; that Narcissus did not run away from home, but was expelled from it for having several times tempted his sister Olympia to sinful acts; that Agesilaos had indeed done away with a superior officer, but because of some squalid wrangle over a woman . . . To say nothing of Saglimbeni, the fraudulency of whose utterances I had already perceived. This showed me that the four of them had not only tricked me, but laughed me to scorn, all their tales being offered me in the form of charades or cryptic ciphers, the ritornello of which was always based on the ambiguity of what is and what seems to be, just as the infinite fancy-dress ball of our life on earth unrolls and unravels . . . And finally leading me on like a child to imagine my quarry the person they wished it to be, at one moment mentioning his impediment of speech and passion for gambling, at another his free access to Court and likeness to Lorenzaccio de' Medici. To the end that, following up all the clues, I easily and of my own accord fell into the trap. A hard blow to my pride; but that smarts less than my remorse at having – in ill-repayment of his favours – done a disservice to my king.

Unless . . . unless by a still more perfidious design those men intended to bequeath a perpetual legacy of terror, inventing a scarecrow to keep us birds away, a non-existent mirage, so constructed that it can in no wise be destroyed. Yes, Your Majesty, my belief is this: that no *God the Father* has ever existed except as a trumped-up bogeyman in their talk; and that they gave the thing such a name out of the merest blasphemy . . .

Your Majesty, oh how everything in my mind is in disarray and all awhirl! Being now well stricken in years, death holds no terrors for me. But I am terrified to find myself the butt of a story I don't understand. I thought I knew those men. I even admired them as the authors of bold and grandiose misdeeds. I admired how with steely hearts they underwent the rigours of their interrogation, and how they mounted the scaffold brave men to the last. Despite the fact that during that last night they were uncertain of themselves as was only human, prompted to hide behind mendacious euphemisms; even though, their lives long, they thought rather of the chains of the poor than of the hunger of the poor; for which I reproached them in the person of Brother Cirillo; with whom, alas – and this is the very extremity of my shame – the moment I disguised myself in his clothes I became imbued to such an extent as often to utter his very words and ape his sentiments . . . Thoroughly warped myself, and all but corrupted by my intercourse with that man, I ask myself, Who am I? We men, who are we? Are we real, or painted figures? Paper metaphors, increate phantoms, non-beings shadowed on the stage of a pantomime of ashes, bubbles blown from the clay pipe of a conjuror who hates us?

If this be so, then nothing is real. Worse still: nothing is. Each and every thing is a zero unable to break free of its own circle. Apocryphal, all of us, but apocryphal also is he who urges or restrains us, who throws us together or tears us apart. We are Carnival snouts attached to skulls, riddled with holes and nullities . . . I saw a picture in Paris a year ago now. It portrayed a monkey in a painter's studio, equipped with palette and brushes. Can this be what we are, we creatures of tears? The scribbles of a daubing monkey? If not, indeed, puppets pendent in the middle of a room and reflected and repeated in two facing mirrors? . . .

Nevertheless, at this hour of moral obscuration in which it seems all things are going to wrack, and every projectile twists aside towards a target of smoke, I cannot imagine why on my lips I find the last words of Christ. I dare not utter them from between my chattering teeth, but, albeit in silence, they serve me as a viaticum for the journey. Not only to impetrate mercy (if one mask can ever have mercy on another mask), but to perfume the inanity of my existence with their fraternal anguish, at the moment when I cast myself into the maw of my non-existence.

Already, indeed, dawn is approaching, I discern it from a

thread of softening blue where the two halves of the curtains are drawn together. The lament of the donkeys now dies down along the shore, and soon the seagulls will return to shriek against the eastern counterscarp, hunting the scraps the cooks throw out each morning. How soon this year has winter come! How I feel its blade run cold along my backbone! The firewood is finished, but in vain do I heap up my books in the hearth. They blacken but they do not warm me, those princes and sorceresses who once lodged there within: Atlante in his castle, Prospero in his cell, Sigismund in his prison . . . Like their pages I shall finish as an ember, in the cackle and stench of blackened matter . . .

In the air I feel a novel silence, as if everyone, prisoners and warders alike, had leave of absence or had made their escape, and I the lone survivor on this forsaken rock. If, for the last time, I turn to look out on the world, between sea and sky I perceive an awe-inspiring blur which, try as I may, I cannot identify. A montgolfier, a cloud, an angel? It brings to mind that tattoo on Agesilaos' arm, which was, he declared, a transfixed butterfly, whereas I maintained that it was a montgolfier, a cloud, an angel, and that we might read a prophecy of flight therein.

But let there be an end to this and to other allegories more captious still. I have nothing more to write, nothing to perform, but the one thing. Nor have I any hope that Mastro Smiriglio will come knocking at my door, hooded, with blood-spattered apron, to offer me the expediency of his hands.

Balestra, or whoever else has the task of laying me out later on, will find my dress uniform folded on the bed: my blue tail-coat, my scarlet trousers, my medals, my busby, my sword . . . The paraments of a priesthood which I persist in proclaiming sacred to the ears of this dumbstruck rock. For all is silent on the island now. Not a cockcrow have I heard this morning, not even the mimicry of one. The breakers are at peace at the foot of the fortress, and the teeth of Mustachio at peace in my head.

Have I dreamt it all up? Am I dreaming it still? As if ready to haul on the rope of a vast stage-curtain of rags, I feel my heartbeats throb in my throat, and am filled with a raging, irrational happiness . . . What if in the mysteries of some super-human alphabet the Omega of darkness into which I am falling were to be the Alpha of an eternal light?

This I will know in an instant, and at the selfsame instant I shall not know that I know it. When, clasping my musket between my knees, one foot on the hammer, the muzzle between my teeth, my head swathed in the king's white standard, I shall hear the crash of the report, like a cry from God, in the silence of the universe.